SCIENCE IS MAGIC
SPELLED BACKWARDS

Borgo Press Books by JACQUELINE LICHTENBERG

THE SIME~GEN SERIES from The Borgo Press

House of Zeor, by Jacqueline Lichtenberg (#1)
Unto Zeor, Forever, by Jacqueline Lichtenberg (#2)
First Channel, by Jean Lorrah and Jacqueline Lichtenberg (#3)
Mahogany Trinrose, by Jacqueline Lichtenberg (#4)
Channel's Destiny, by Jean Lorrah and Jacqueline Lichtenberg (#5)
RenSime, by Jacqueline Lichtenberg (#6)
Ambrov Keon, by Jean Lorrah (#7)
Zelerod's Doom, by Jacqueline Lichtenberg and Jean Lorrah (#8)
Personal Recognizance, by Jacqueline Lichtenberg (#9)
The Story Untold and Other Stories, by Jean Lorrah (#10)
To Kiss or to Kill, by Jean Lorrah (#11)
The Farris Channel, by Jacqueline Lichtenberg (#12)

Other Jacqueline Lichtenberg Borgo Press Books:

City of a Million Legends
Molt Brother
Science Is Magic Spelled Backwards and Other Stories (Jacqueline Lichtenberg Collected, Book One) (ed. by Jean Lorrah)
Through the Moon Gate and Other Tales of Vampirism (Jacqueline Lichtenberg Collected, Book Two) (ed. by Jean Lorrah)

SCIENCE IS MAGIC SPELLED BACKWARDS

AND OTHER STORIES: JACQUELINE LICHTENBERG COLLECTED, BOOK ONE

JACQUELINE

LICHTENBERG

Edited by Jean Lorrah

THE BORGO PRESS

MMXI

SCIENCE IS MAGIC SPELLED BACKWARDS

FIRST EDITION

Published by Wildside Press LLC

www.wildsidebooks.com

DEDICATION

For John Betancourt at Wildside Press

and

Robert Reginald at Borgo Press,

Who had the idea to collect my short stories

CONTENTS

ACKNOWLEDGMENTS

THESE STORIES WERE previously published as follows, and are reprinted (with minor editing, updating, and textual modifications) by permission of the author:

"Recompense" was first published in *Galileo*, #2, 1977. Copyright © 1976 by Avenue Victor Hugo; Copyright © 2011 by Jacqueline Lichtenberg.

"The Vanillamint Tapestry" was first published in *Cassandra Rising*, edited by Isaac Asimov and Alice Laurance, Doubleday & Co., 1978. Copyright © 1978 by Isaac Asimov and Alice Laurance; Copyright © 2011 by Jacqueline Lichtenberg.

"Science Is Magic Spelled Backwards" was first published in *Hecate's Cauldron*, edited by Susan M. Shwartz, DAW Books, 1982. Copyright © 1982 by Susan M. Shwartz; Copyright © 2011 by Jacqueline Lichtenberg.

"Event at Holiday Rock" was first published in *Speculations*, edited by Isaac Asimov and Alice Laurance, Houghton-Mifflin, 1982. Copyright © 1982 by Isaac Asimov and Alice Laurance; Copyright © 2011 by Jacqueline Lichtenberg.

"Aventura" was first published in *Marion Zimmer*

Personal Acknowledgments 2011

First I must thank Ronnie Bob Whitaker. Without his computer wizardry retrieving old files, scanning and OCR'ing typescript and copies, most of this work would not be available.

But he has an even more astonishing talent to the chronically disorganized—he keeps marvelous files!

Karen MacLeod is also much better than I at filing, and can't be left out of these acknowledgements. She has done more than can ever be listed to keep me organized.

Sharon Jarvis has put time, effort and skill into crafting the presentation of these volumes of collected stories.

And I have to thank the editors who originally solicited these stories from me. Most of them would never have been written had I not been asked for a certain number of words about a certain topic!

Robert Reginald, formerly (and presently) of Borgo

Press, remembered me and gave both me and Jean Lorrah the opportunity to get these stories back into print. His advice will be treasured.

EDITOR'S INTRODUCTION

BY JEAN LORRAH

One well-known definition of science fiction is "the literature of ideas." If there is any science fiction writer whose work fits that definition, it is Jacqueline Lichtenberg. She creates whole universes at the drop of a hat, drawing not only from her background in chemistry, but from all the sciences, history, geography, religion, myth, the Kaballah, the Tarot, and Astrology.

Out of this heady mix, Jacqueline has created a kind of unified field theory that underlies her body of work. The only problem is, it would take a lifetime to sort it all out of the hints she drops in her stories. I haven't known Jacqueline for an entire lifetime yet, but we have been friends and collaborators for thirty years.

Jacqueline and I met through *Star Trek* fandom. We both wrote items for *Spockanalia,* the first Trek fanzine, but truth be told, I did not pick her name out of the rest of the contributors at that point. It was when I published my own Trek fanzine, *The Night of the Twin Moons,* that one of my readers sent me a copy of Jacqueline's first published novel, *House of Zeor.* Now *that* made me sit up and take notice!

House of Zeor introduced me to the Sime~Gen universe, a complex world in which very little is what it first appears. What made me read the book twice in one weekend, though, was the intimate adventure between the two main characters. Here was the kind of relationship story that I usually had to go hunting for in mainstream literature, united with my favorite genre, science fiction. It was a combination I wanted to write myself—and here was someone who had already done it.

I was at that time early in my teaching career, and thus far all my professional publications were nonfiction. So I wrote a review of *House of Zeor,* and sent it off to a Trek fanzine, knowing that this was exactly the kind of story Trek fans would love. The review was not a total rave, though—I pointed out the flaws, which were typical of a first novel, but in no way reduced the emotional impact of the story.

To my surprise, Jacqueline wrote to me (it was still the age of snailmail) to ask if she could reprint my review in *Ambrov Zeor,* the first Sime~Gen fanzine. Through our subsequent correspondence, she found out that I was an English Professor. The next thing I knew, a huge, heavy box arrived on my doorstep: her latest draft of *Unto Zeor, Forever!* This was raw Jacqueline, even more emotionally powerful than her first novel, but untamed and, in that condition, unpublishable. I wrote all over it, and added pages of explanations—I probably wrote as many words as were contained in the manuscript—and sent it back to her, not knowing what to expect.

What I got was a sincere thank you—Jacqueline is one of those rare people who genuinely appreciates constructive criticism. She then proceeded to address all the problems I had pointed out in her rewrite—but resolving each in a completely different way from what I had suggested.

And that incident pretty well sums up Jacqueline: she always does the unexpected, in both her writing and her life. For instance, the next correspondence we had was over the question of how the channels, featured in the Sime~Gen universe as a given, could ever have figured out how to channel. I kept making suggestions, which she shot down, until finally I came up with a scenario that would work—which she promptly sold to her publisher as *First Channel* by Jean Lorrah and Jacqueline Lichtenberg!

As you read the stories in this collection, be prepared for both unique characters and different turns of plot. Jacqueline rarely does what you expect—and that is one of her most endearing traits.

Jean Lorrah
Murray, Kentucky
2010

FOREWORD

These stories do not represent my style or skill as of 2010.

This volume presents the stories in chronological order as they were written—not the usual way an anthology is arranged.

Many of the lessons I teach at writing seminars and in the online writing school, WorldCrafters Guild at simegen.com, and on blogs are not exemplified here because this is where I learned those lessons.

Nevertheless, the underlying concepts, themes and subject matter are very much a part of my development as a writer.

"Recompense" is about a human/alien friendship that involves the human compensating for the alien's biological imperatives. That could easily describe the two novels, *Molt Brother* and *City of a Million Legends* now available in reprint at Wildside Press and in e-book.

"The Vanillamint Tapestry" is still one of my own favorites, for it deals with aliens who have a totally different view of reality—so different that though they exist in our world, they do their living in another. This story plays with visions of God, and I'm continuing to do that in all my work.

"Recompense" and "Vanillamint Tapestry" applied what I'd learned creating the *Kraith Universe* stories (*Star Trek* Fan Fiction done in the 1970's and now posted for free reading at simegen.com). There were about fifty creative contributors to the *Kraith Universe*. I used the responses to those stories as research for the Bantam Paperback, *Star Trek Lives!* by Jacqueline Lichtenberg, Sondra Marshak, and Joan Winston.

In *Kraith*, I invented my first trisexual aliens and created a relationship between one of them and Kirk and Spock.

From the beginning, my writing has always been about how relationships (not always romance, but all sorts of bonded relationships) influences actions, changes people, pressures them to soul-growth, reveals hidden possibilities, and generally rules existence.

But beyond that, I've focused on just one of the many possibilities that Relationship brings to a story or a life. Trust.

If the Relationship is adversarial, trust is based on an understanding of the other person such that predicted responses in any situation materialize.

"Science Is Magic Spelled Backwards," which I updated with a few terms without changing a single scene also challenges the ordinary view of the universe.

One point of fascination to me has always been how someone raised in a household with one view can grow up to see the world very differently, to understand the nature of what is real—and what is not!—in a way their parents just can't.

Child/Parent and Parent/Child are another pair of Relationships that drive the conflicts at the core of our lives.

"Event at Holiday Rock" is an ultra-short written specifically to break into a wholly different style than I'd ever employed. That was the requirement for the anthology it was solicited for. Make up your own mind if it succeeded, and if that newer style affected what was written after.

"Aventura" was written at request of Marion Zimmer Bradley for her *Fantasy Magazine*, and won a reader's poll award. As a result it was reprinted in the mass market paperback *Best of Marion Zimmer Bradley's Fantasy Magazine* which also got translated into German.

"A Mother's Curse" is the first chapter of what I'd hoped would become a novel—and didn't. Again, I find I become absorbed in looking at reality from a different view.

"Ruella and the Stone" is new, but a rather introverted experimental story. One woman goes alone into a cave and learns something about herself that changes everything. It's a close focus on a mystical initiation.

So even a person's Relationship with herself can drive a life's story.

For me, the key to all Relationship is Intimacy.

Over the years, I found that I seriously dislike "Action" genre stories—though as a writer, I truly appreciate well written ones. Personally, I don't think that "Action" can ever solve a problem at the level that satisfies me.

And stories are always about people who have problems—when the problem of a lifetime falls on your head, you are in the portion of your life when your story is happening.

As you can see from the stories in this volume, I look for solutions not in "Action" (*i.e.* hitting people, blowing things up, using force, power or duplicity to neutralize an opponent, though such things are done and happen to characters) but rather in "Intimacy"—the kind of relationship between the character and other characters, between the character and the universe, or between the character and him/herself, that brings trust into life.

As I sold more stories and novels in the Science Fiction and Fantasy genre, I was taught that SF/F is Action Adventure, and if your plot is not Action/Adventure, it won't sell.

Well, a few writers managed to violate that maxim and win awards, but by and large most SF/F published in the mid-twentieth century was Action/Adventure.

Even *Star Trek*, the first and for many years only SF on TV, was formulated as Action/Adventure.

But as I studied what the fans did with *Star Trek* in the early fanzines, I realized they were wrenching the *Star Trek* Universe around into the shape that I most prefer—but they had no name for what they were doing.

Meanwhile, my study of the genre led me to the conclusion that Science Fiction is not a genre at all. As I learned all the formulae for other genres, I realized you can write any other genre in Science Fiction—because Science Fiction isn't a genre—it is Literature.

So I set out to write a novel in each of the genres that exist, setting them all in my Sime~Gen Universe. After only two novels were published in Sime~Gen, Jean Lorrah jumped in and began adding Relationship driven stories, love stories and romances. And we've been working at it ever since.

At the same time, I was also writing novels in other series. In the mid-1980's I won the Romantic Times Award for best SF writer with my novel *Dushau*, the first novel in a trilogy (*Dushau*, *Farfetch*, *Outreach*, now available on Kindle). It is an SF/Romance, driven by a human/alien Relationship.

I have several vampire universes, too, containing both SF and Fantasy vampires who have a tendency to form tight, intimate bonds with humans.

Studying what I write—and what I enjoy most in films and books—and what Star Trek fans and fans of other television shows write in their fan fiction, I found that there is a common thread binding all this work together.

I decided that what we're doing is inventing a new genre. We replace the "Action" in Action/Adventure with Intimacy.

I named this hidden genre Intimate Adventure.

In Intimate/Adventure combat and the heroism is on

the field of emotional bonding, not physical bashing.

Such emotional bonds can only form when both parties have the courage to drop their emotional defenses and stand stripped weaponless on the emotional battlefield.

Problems are solved by combining disparate entities via bonds of trust—the necessary precursor of love. The biggest barrier to that combination is disparate views of reality, the meat of my writing from the beginning.

After years of arguing about the parameters of what constitutes Intimate/Adventure and what to call it, Jean Lorrah and I were approached by a publishing company to write a book on this Hidden Genre.

We got together on AIM to discuss the outline. At one point, we stopped, stumped. We couldn't prove that Intimate/Adventure is a genre.

Then Jean said that Intimate/Adventure is in fact not a genre at all—it is an Archetype.

We rewrote the outline and submitted the book proposal, which was quickly rejected. It wasn't a book on genre, so they had no place for it.

We are now presenting Intimate Adventure as a plot-archetype with a distinctive signature of its own. It isn't something the fanfic writers invented, or that I promulgated. It has existed since the dawn of time, and in fact has long since become one of Hollywood's favorite archetypes.

But it's never been sorted out and given a distinctive name of its own, a label you can use to find more of it, until now. Intimate Adventure is the name of what I write, and even my earliest stories bear that imprint, long before I knew what I was doing.

You'll find updates and more about what I'm doing now, the Sime~Gen universe novels with Jean Lorrah, other new and reprint novels in e-book, and new non-fiction, plus links to writing craft blogs all at simegen. com. For a summary of currently available titles and free chapters see http://jacquelinelichtenberg.com—or just Google my name.

Jacqueline Lichtenberg
Arizona
2010

RECOMPENSE

Maxwell Dameus Fenton, III, drew himself to his full six feet and allowed his ample paunch to add to the dominance that was more than dignity. He took a deep breath as he eyed the Reservations Clerk and the Liner Captain and then pitched his voice low and spoke with a dangerously intense calm, "I will not, repeat not, under any circumstances share a cabin with a non-human. My stockholders would never stand for it. As humans, you should understand that."

"But, Mr. Fenton," the lean, grizzled Captain said, "I assure you our professional discretion is irreproachable."

"I'm certain it is. But you do carry other passengers."

Bolstering his confidence by brushing his fingers over the computer input controls on his gleaming counter, the clerk said, "Mr. Fenton, the Line deeply regrets your inconvenience and will go to any lengths to compensate you for losses due to the delay if you choose not to share with our previous passenger, but the law doesn't allow us to bump this passenger."

"The Law! You know damned well you make the

law on these forsaken transfer stations! And the entire worth of your Line couldn't cover the losses IDC will sustain if I don't get to Samonhauk on time! The economies of whole solar systems will rock to the blow."

"Sir." The Captain stepped around the counter with one professional hand outstretched. "Won't you just come aboard and meet the other passenger? Right this way. It won't take but a moment."

Fenton allowed his caped arm to be cradled as the shorter man guided him. "All right. If you people haven't the nerve, I'll go evict him myself!" He freed himself, brushed wrinkles from his impeccably tailored business suit, and marched beside the Captain out into the cavernous Round Room that was the central chamber of the hollow asteroid, over the teeming causeway and up the slideway to one of the higher ports.

The ship corridors were narrow, quiet, and amply supplied with railings, outer viewscreens and the showcased artworks of various races, but the passengers they passed were all human. Eventually, they rounded a curve and entered the first class deck, which differed from the rest of the accommodations only in allowing an extra nine cubic feet per passenger. The Presidential Suite boasted an extra twelve cubic feet.

The Captain brushed the signal plate set into the rectangular door and after a slight pause it clicked outward invitingly. The "suite" consisted of one large room with two chests-of-drawers and a table with two chairs. In the wall to their right, a door stood ajar revealing gleaming sanitary facilities.

The colors were neutral beiges and grays and there was no attempt at decoration lest some dignitary be offended. The dim lighting concealed whatever contrasts in tone and texture the designers had employed to relieve the monotony. Fenton observed, privately, that bon voyage gifts had a place in such a room and were conspicuously absent now.

As they entered, a gray drape swished aside on power-pulls, and at the same instant Fenton shivered in the chill, dry air that reeked of bread mold and knew who the Presidential Suite belonged to.

The Captain said, "Mr. Fenton, may I present Mr. Zepon Aamidtsurras. Mr. Aamidtsurras, may I present Mr. Fenton, the man who claims this cabin, as I've explained."

The Stilhzani reclining on the bed was living proof that the phyla of one planet can't be compared to those of another. The patches of feathery growths on the round, earless skull weren't avian. The neck frill, prominent incisors and scaly skin texture weren't reptilian. The slanted, glowing eyes with the paired, vertical pupil slits weren't feline. To sophisticated eyes, he was comfortably humanoid, though with twice as many joints to his limbs.

Fenton's eyes were more than sophisticated. They flicked from the motley, light green fuzz that should be blue to the shiny green skin that should be dull and met the glazed, listless red eyes set far apart in the all too human face. He didn't need the bread mold body odor to tell him the Stilhzani's condition was truly critical.

Zepon said, "Forgive that I not rise." His accent, while surprisingly intelligible, ignored Terran vowel-consonant distinctions with fine abandon.

As the shock wore off, Fenton knew what he had to do and he did it without hesitation. He touched the backs of his hands to his eyes and then swept them outward in the Stilhzani gesture that said, "I humbly beg permission to share your abode for a space of time short but definite."

Some of the glazed look faded as Zepon said, "Why would you believe I willing to share with a human?"

"I don't," said Fenton, allowing the anger to rise in him, the same anger that had propelled him through a brilliant career ending prematurely as a colonel in the Federation Force of Order, the same anger that was now about to abbreviate his career in business. It was a cold anger that struck a paralyzing chill through the heart of all who encountered it. He said, "However, you obviously aren't going to make it without help."

He turned to the Captain. "Have the purser get me several changes of warmer clothing, then stow my baggage and get this glorified garbage scow moving. I'll no longer tolerate a moment's delay. Move!"

The Captain retreated hastily, not at all sure what had caused the sudden reversal but not inclined to question his good fortune.

Fenton closed the door and went to examine the thermostat set in the wall beside the door. He spun the scales until he found Fahrenheit and read sixty-five. He adjusted it to sixty-two, and then turned back to Zepon, his face a stone setting for implacable gray eyes. "I'll bet you haven't been out of that bed for days."

"Truth. But what do you know of it?"

"I know that it's twenty-two standard days to Stilhza and that you're going to live through every last one of those days. You're going to hate me, but you're going to live because I will not, repeat not, travel on the same ship with a corpse. Is that understood?"

Without waiting for acknowledgement, Fenton took the three strides to the other bed, flung his cloak onto it, and rounded on the Stilhzani. "What I want to know is how you came to be here in this condition and why nobody has been helping you."

"And what would you know of 'this condition'!?"

Approaching the recumbent figure with bitter determination, Fenton said, "I know enough. Now roll over." Warming one hand against the other palm, Fenton looked down into the now clear scarlet eyes with their paired, yellow pupils open to the dim lighting. He wasn't disturbed by the eyes. In fact, he was pleased to note they were now clearly focused on him. That was an encouraging sign.

Something in him melted and he leaned down to speak softly. "Listen, Zepon, I know enough to recognize incipient estivation when I see it. Now, it's going to be a long three weeks home for you and you just aren't going to make it if you don't get some attention." He laid a hand on the Stilhzani's shoulder, carefully clear of the sensitive frill. "I know how to do this, believe me. I won't hurt you. Now roll over."

Too enervated to put up a fight, Zepon rolled over to expose his bare back to the human's touch. With a deft gentleness surprising in those large, blunt fingers, Fenton probed the lower back until he found the upper emission orifice. It was retracted and hard as stone. He laughed. "Relax. You're tense enough to start spewing your wrapping right now, and that would be both futile and fatal." He patted the barely distended abdomen briefly. "You haven't got what it takes yet."

For several minutes he crooned soothing words and massaged the orifice and the whole back while Zepon emitted hoarse groans and occasionally twitched away, gasping. Finally, Fenton said, "There, that's better. Doesn't hurt so much now, does it?"

"Yes. You've done well. I believe I could actually sleep."

"Oh, now, none of that. Come on, roll over." When he had him on his back again, he gripped both those hands with their seven long, four-jointed fingers and two opposable thumbs. "Here, I'll help you sit up."

"No. Let me rest."

"You're going to take a walk."

"I can't...."

"I know. But you're going to anyway." He hauled the limp body to a sitting position, swung the thin but powerful legs to the floor. "Now, stand up. I won't let go, I promise."

He draped Zepon's arm over his shoulders, settling both elbows comfortably and lifted him to his feet. The Stilhzani was easily as tall as Fenton, much thinner, but, Fenton knew, ordinarily much stronger than any human.

For ten minutes, he walked Zepon around the room until the Stilhzani could manage some semblance of coordination. "OK, that's enough for the first time." He deposited his charge on the bed and made him comfortable. "Wait right here and don't go to sleep."

Fenton went into the tiny washroom, found a cup, filled it, and returned to shake the Stilhzani to wakefulness. "Here, drink this."

"What is it?"

"Just water."

"No. I couldn't, I'd...." He made a little circular motion with his hand.

"I know, I'll get something." He drew him to a sitting position and handed him the cup. "Drink. I'll be right back." He rummaged around in the washroom a second time and came back with a large pan just in time to brace Zepon's head as the retching started. The water came up first, followed by great quantities of green mucus, until Fenton was wondering if the pan would be big enough. Then the heaving became drier and finally subsided.

"OK, now you can take a little nap until the food arrives."

"Oh, please, no. I'll be sick again."

"Not this time. I think you got it all up. How long has it been since you've eaten?"

"I really don't know."

"Figures. I'll find out from the steward and order

something appropriate. If you're not sure, though, you could try some more water."

"No, thank you." Zepon slumped back, exhausted.

Fenton slipped out of the room quietly, blinking against the bright corridor lights. Inhaling the clean air gratefully, he followed the strands of coffee aroma to their steward's station.

Twenty minutes later, he returned with a well-stocked tray and shook Zepon awake. "You told them to leave you alone, so they did."

Managing to sit up without assistance, Zepon regarded his benefactor levelly. "I wonder how you learned all this."

"Eat something, you'll feel better. Then we'll talk. For three weeks, we'll talk." Fenton settled the tray over Zepon's lap. "Well, are you going to eat or do I have to feed you?"

Zepon peeked under some of the bright covers, eyed Fenton and performed the frill-rippling equivalent of a shrug. "I can try."

It took him half an hour to nibble at everything and eat about a third of a bowl of the soup. In the meantime, the Chief Steward arrived with Fenton's luggage and several changes of heavier clothing.

When he finished stowing his belongings, Fenton heard the warning chime for the warp drive and sat down on his bunk to wait it out. "Here we go, Zepon. Can you hang onto that tray?"

"Yes. I'm feeling stronger for the moment."

Then the wrenching twist that was not a movement

but a distortion surged through them. It was short and very mild since this was a modern passenger vessel boasting all the latest refinements. Afterwards, Fenton put the tray on the table and took a chair to Zepon's bed.

"Fine. Now tell me, how the devil did you get yourself into this mess?"

"I'm most curious to know how you learned such skills. Are you, perhaps, a physician?"

"No. A friend taught me."

"I never adequately can repay you for your efforts."

"I'm not asking payment."

"The more pity that your efforts will be useless."

"My efforts are never, repeat never, useless."

"To survive this, it is necessary to have a strong desire to live. Obviously, I lack sufficient will."

"Why?"

Zepon's neck frill plastered itself against his shoulders, clearly indicating this was a private matter. Fenton abandoned that tack, knowing the Stilhzani attitude toward privacy.

"All right. Your name is Zepon and you're of the Aamidtsurraa Quadrant. How did you get this 'suite'?"

"It's the only room aboard with sufficiently flexible environmental controls."

Fenton nodded. "Of course. And this was the only transport available. That's really all I need to know. A man in my position has the means of acquiring information."

Zepon looked again at this huge man with the

so-gentle hands and the so-implacable will. "You are the President of the Intersystem Development Corporation?"

"Right. But call me Max."

"How is it a person of your position knows so much about Stilhzani?"

"I told you, I had a friend."

"Do you also know that if it gets much colder in here it may throw me into hibernation...or worse?"

"It's not that cold. You're just getting stiff. Come on. Time for your walk."

"No. I can't."

"On your feet." Fenton pushed his chair back and held out an arm. When Zepon didn't respond, he moved him bodily but un-protesting onto rubbery legs. "For the next three weeks, you're not going to sleep more than four hours at a time, you're going to eat, and exercise, and you're going to hate every minute of it. Especially later, but I'm not going to let you wrap yourself up until you're safely home. Now that's my final word on the subject. Understood?"

It was then that Zepon knew that he was going to live whether he liked it or not. And, being in no condition to care much, he didn't fight the idea. When Fenton helped him back to bed, Zepon fell into a deep sleep.

Satisfied, the human welcomed the opportunity to slip out to the dining room for a meal.

A week passed under Fenton's severe regimen and Zepon seemed to be holding his own, but in the second week, the lethargy returned and his protests, while feeble, became more frequent.

Fenton spent much of his time brooding over the mess he'd made of his life by adopting another Stilhzani. But he wasted no time on regrets, preferring to plan a job hunting campaign while mentally calculating his cash assets.

Then, one day near the end of the week, Fenton roused his charge for a meal and afterwards had it abruptly returned to him. When he'd cleaned up the mess and pulled up a chair to sit beside the recumbent Stilhzani, Zepon said, "I'm sorry."

"There's no need to apologize. We've done well so far. We're going to make it." Fenton gauged Zepon's growing abdomen and body odor. "You're first quarter of your Quadrant, aren't you?"

Zepon's neck frill flushed violet in assent. "I've always been among the first to retire into estivation."

"All right. So you can't eat any more. I can understand that. The Aamidtsurraa Quadrant passes into High Season tomorrow, if my calculations are correct. The catacombs have been filling with first comers for days. I don't dare lower the temperature in here any further. In fact, I should start raising it soon to avoid upsetting your natural rhythm more than necessary. You've been feeling the chill lately."

That last was such a flat statement of fact that Zepon half raised his head to train all four pupils on his benefactor. "You have lived on Stilhza. How else could you know so much?"

Fenton studied his fingernails meticulously. "I...ah...

have an unusually high empathy rating."

Zepon allowed his head to fall back to the pillow. "That does explain-not how you learned so much about Stilhza when most humans know-not that we exist, and care-not."

"I told you, I had a friend."

"Why are you doing this...for me?"

"Because it needs to be done."

"Why? What difference in your Totality that I exist or not?"

This gave Fenton pause. Why did it matter to him whether this insignificant individual called Zepon lived or died?

"Max." Zepon's soft voice called Fenton out of introspection. "Tell me about your friend."

Something in Zepon's tone, some gentle prodding or need pierced the cyst that had encased that memory for so many years, and like an abscess draining, the story spilled out of him.

"I'd just gotten an emergency field promotion to Lieutenant Colonel and command of a Post out by the Orion Wedge. I'd been promoted too far too fast and the responsibility was really more than I could handle. I was Earth born and about as segregationist as they come. You can imagine my reaction when Khela'an Aamidtsurraa introduced himself as my aide and proceeded to run the Post while I foundered about trying to become oriented.

"At the time, he was a Captain, but you know how much that means for a nonhuman. He was a twenty-year man and he had more experience in his seventh finger than I'd had in my entire life. And at that, he was still a young Stilhzani.

"It took many bitter humiliations to knock some sense into me, but I finally realized which of us was the ranking officer and eventually we became fast friends. He made an officer-and-a-gentleman out of me as the Academy hadn't, and I owed him my life and my career many times over.

"Then one day, orders arrived saying there would be a delay in his hibernation leave. Oh, I sent in emergency pleas, all the usual paperwork, even sent some precedent-smashing tunnelgrams to Hub Central. But you know how the Service is. It was a wretched three weeks later before transport arrived.

"I insisted on accompanying him home. We made it that time. I really don't know how. He was first quarter too.

"All in all, those were good years. He got me a promotion and I got him a promotion and by some miracle I kept him on my staff everywhere I went. And, through the years, I leaned about the difficulties Stilhzani have away from their natural environment, and I even learned something of that natural environment.

"Then, one year, we didn't make it." Fenton sat on that bald statement for a long time and Zepon let him brood in silence. Finally, Fenton took a deep breath symbolic of the fresh determination that had come to him as grief receded. "So I resigned my commission to do something to realign the structure of our society before it topples from being human heavy.

"It was really an accident that I fell into Intersystem Development, but I took the opportunity to find a way to enable other races to colonize as extensively as humanity has. Of all the races that are bound to their planets, the Stilhzani are in the worst position. At least individuals of other races can travel freely if they've the inclination.

"The Stilhzani have the inclination, but it's too dangerous for the average person to consider. The Stilhzani need help the most, and are a potentially profitable market. But it's been ten years, and our labs still haven't come up with anything commercial. Until now. Perhaps.

"I was on my way to an important conference on the matter when I found that my reservation had been picked up by someone else. I was too furious to even ask who or why. And when I met you, of course I had no choice but to help."

He was interrupted by the door chime. He pushed the release and walked toward the door. The steward stood at a crisp attention and, tight-lipped, handed Fenton the tunnelgram. Fenton nodded and closed the door before he broke the computer's seal, skipped the salutation and read the words printed on the glossy:

As Chairman of the Board, it is my duty to inform you that there must be no scandal involving any official of this Corporation. I must remind you of the terms of your contract which

was written with a view to your past prefer-
ences.

Respectfully,

Folding the sheet carefully, Fenton tucked it away among his things before resuming his seat.

"What was that?

"Nothing important."

"Tunnelgrams are never unimportant."

"Just business."

"Expensive business."

Fenton nodded. "Yes, very. It's time for your walk."

"So you want to save my life to compensate for Khela'an's loss."

"You're a student of human psychology?"

Zepon copied Fenton's tone. "Humans have a monopoly on guilt?"

"Not guilt. Avarice."

Zepon's neck frill fluttered a question mark.

Fenton translated. "Greed. If I let you die so I could get to a conference, would any Stilhzani ever deal with my company?"

"Probably. After a while. Not am I important."

"Every living soul is important. Enough procrastinating. On your feet."

As he allowed Fenton to haul him erect, Zepon said, "Why do you believe we have soul?"

"That's not for me to judge. It's enough you're alive."

The lethargy reclaimed Zepon and Fenton's answer echoed in his uncomprehending mind. As they neared the washroom on their third circuit, Zepon veered off, saying, "Max, I think I'm going to be sick again."

Fenton helped him silently, sponged off his face, and carried him back to the bed, knowing that from then on, he'd have a bed patient on his hands.

The next five days passed in a long series of crises with Zepon's lucid moments becoming shorter and wider spaced. Between jobs, Fenton's mind kept returning to the 'gram that really said, "Move away from that Stilhzani or you're fired."

With each passing hour, such a course became even more impossible as his minute by minute attendance was the only thing keeping Zepon from giving up. After all, IDC was only a job.

But, finally, when they were forty hours out of Stilhza, Fenton had to slip out to send a tunnelgram ahead. He stood at the counter, under the cold eye of the human clerk, and laboriously blocked in the Stilhzani characters he hadn't used for ten years, paid for it out of his own pocket, and hurried back to his charge, knowing what the clerk thought of him but not the slightest concerned.

When the door clicked open on the musty dimness he'd grown accustomed to, he knew at once that something was wrong. He'd been raising the temperature and humidity gradually for days, until the room was stuffy for him but frigid to the heat-starved Stilhzani. But now it seemed warmer than when he'd left, even ignoring the cloying moldiness that permeated everything.

Swiftly, he checked the thermostat and turned it down a hair before he went to his charge. Zepon was curled with the small of his back to the wall and his head tucked between his arms at an angle impossible for a human. Fenton gasped, and let the shock of failure wash through him as it had ten years ago.

But ten years ago he'd been too late. This time, he knew Zepon had had no more than fifteen minutes to bond himself in place. He'd stopped breathing, but he hadn't yet begun to spew the gelatinous wrapping material that now fully distended his abdomen. There was still a good chance.

Carefully avoiding the sensitive neck frill, Fenton grasped the Stilhzani's shoulders and gently but insistently pulled him away from the wall. The transparent rope of connective tissue elongated until Fenton could see it hadn't hardened into the nearly indestructible anchor it would become. Then it broke away from the wall with a wet smack and slowly retracted into the lower orifice.

The upper orifice had just begun to project itself as Fenton hauled the compacted body to the edge of the bed and laboriously unfolded the limbs to get him in position for artificial respiration. He stripped off his watch, set it on the bed, clambered astride the head, and for the first time in years regretting his respectable paunch, he began the rhythmic pumping. Soon he was rewarded with a trickle of blue-green mucus that became a gushing flood and then Zepon was coughing and gasping.

Hastily, Fenton hauled him to his feet and slapped his face smartly until those glowing red eyes focused on him, but without recognition. Zepon pulled away from the human, neck frill plastered down, blue with revulsion.

"It's Max Fenton, Zepon, try to remember. It's not time yet. We're still aboard ship."

Memory returned but anger grew. "By what right?!" Shaking, he spat fiercely, "Get away from me...*human!*"

Fenton retreated a few steps. "Now calm down, Zepon. I'm sorry I had to do that, but it's only a matter of hours to Stilhza. If you think what I did was bad, imagine what it would be like to wake up alone, not a female within parsecs, presuming of course you could wake up. And if that isn't enough, remember the Line would have you removed and no court would call it murder."

Slowly, Fenton saw sense return to those blazing eyes and he urged the Stilhzani into a chair. "Now, just sit still. I'll fix the bed." He swung into the familiar routine of cleaning up a mess and, as he worked, he said, "It wasn't your fault. Some defect in the thermostat caused the temperature to rise suddenly while I was out. It wasn't much, but in your condition—"

Installed between clean sheets, Zepon said, "I'm sorry I was angry. I was confused."

"Forget it. I know how you felt."

Those eyes focused in a rare moment of complete lucidity. "But how do your people feel about what you're doing?"

"Oh, the human race disowned me years ago. Doesn't bother me."

"You may be a Corporation President, but you're still just an employee. You'll be fired."

Fenton noted how the anger-induced vitality improved Zepon's accent as well as his mental agility. "If you die, I'll certainly lose everything I've built these last ten years. But if you live, maybe I can salvage something. It might improve my position vastly if I knew how you'd come to be in this predicament."

"I guess I owe you that much." Zepon's frill rose briefly in a gesture accepting the human into his inner-most circle of friends and Fenton flowed with a warmth he hadn't know since Khela'an had accepted him.

The Stilhzani drew a breath, coughed raggedly, and said, "A year ago, I got about two hundred of us together for an attempt to colonize Stovain VI, a planet out on the far frontier of the Federation."

"Strange I hadn't heard of it."

Zepon's neck frill fluttered annoyance. "I found private funds. I planned to establish a bretalon planta-tion. The planet was suitable, and since bretalon is one pharmaceutical that only grows on Stilhza and seems to respond only to Stilhzani hands, the market on that edge of the Federation is brisk.

"We found a location that seemed ideal. There was a large, active volcano whose lower skirts were riddled with delightful catacombs. The outside temperature wouldn't stabilize sufficiently, but the caves were well heated. So we installed vents to tame the volcano, planted our crops and were very optimistic as the temperature rose through the season quite comfortably.

"Then one night, the volcano blew up, vents and all. In the end, I was the only survivor. I stayed at the Service's District Hospital until my...wife...died. I didn't really care whether they put me on this ship or not. I still don't really care whether I live or how I die."

Fenton whistled tunelessly between even white teeth. He knew the deep attachment implied by Zepon's term, wife. Not a sex partner but a life partner. With estivation approaching, of course he'd lost the will to live. But this was a real break!

"Would you be willing to try that project again? This time with professional backing?"

"I have not will."

"Not now. But when you wake up—" Fenton was counting on the tremendous personality shifts so characteristic of the Stilhzani after their severe seasonal changes.

"I'm not going to live through this."

"Get that nonsense out of your head! I won't stand for it. We're only a few hours out of Stilhza. I've just 'grammed the Aamidst to expect you and I am not, repeat not, going to let you make a liar out of me!"

But the lucidity was fading and Fenton knew that from now on, he'd get no sleep at all.

If the week had been arduous, the following hours were hell. Fenton had to content himself with fighting a delaying action, giving in gracefully when it was no longer possible to forestall the inevitable. Several times Zepon's labored breathing ceased and, swallowing his heart, Fenton pumped air into the mucus-filled lungs and bore Zepon's increasing hatred with calm indifference. He knew that if he lived, Zepon would be cheerfully thankful.

During the rare moments of inaction, Fenton kept himself awake by rehearsing the defense of his actions. He was sure he could sell the Stovain VI project, if only he could keep Zepon alive. The Board was composed of men whose sole motivation was making money. They'd condone anything if there was a clear profit in it. With an experienced leader, a colony just might succeed.

Eventually, Fenton stopped watching the clock and just conquered each minute separately. He convinced himself that the nightmare would go on forever and counted each choked breath a victory and each muttered curse a triumph. He talked himself hoarse alternating quiet encouragement with acid-tipped jibes at Zepon's pride, couched in the remains of his spoken Stilhzani.

The door chime, when it came, was an unexpected shock to fatigue-deadened nerves. He palmed the lock button and forced himself to his feet as the four Stilhzani rescue workers entered with their bubble stretcher.

They brushed the human aside and went quietly to work, handling the patient with sympathetic expertness. In moments, they'd transferred the groaning and gasping Zepon to the stretcher and as the others departed, one of them came over to Fenton.

"Not have we met before?" asked the Stilhzani, searching Fenton's stubbled chin with double-pupiled eyes.

Fenton smoothed back his hair, oddly conscious of its increasing thinness. "Yes, we have. Many years ago, I had a friend—"

"Yesss." The Stilhzani's neck frill flushed purple in assent. "I remember Khela'an. You now have a new friend?"

"Possibly. But at the moment he hates me."

"You will speak with him later."

"Of course. I understand."

"I must go."

"Sleep warmly," Fenton called after the swiftly retreating back, making a mental note to brush up on his spoken Stilhzani. It seemed he was going to need it.

THE VANILLAMINT
TAPESTRY

Raymond Yost didn't like the idea of working on loan to the Intelligence Agency. He was a scholar, not a spy. But his feet carried him relentlessly along the springy floored, brightly utilitarian corridor toward the Vesting Chamber. He turned the last corner, squared his bony shoulders, and paced the final fifty yards with thin-lipped determination.

He didn't like the idea of working so close to a partner's fission time either, but he'd keep his word, even if it killed him...and it probably would.

He'd said that many times in the last nine years, and each time he'd survived. Director Proken kept saying that experience would polish his technique, but, privately, Yost thought experience would polish him off. He'd never had the nerve to try the pun on the bald-headed, blue-skinned Director of Humanoid Correlationists.

At twenty-nine, all Yost had to show for his life's work was an Interplanetary Health Certificate claiming that his six-foot, hundred-fifty-pound, Terran-born body was in excellent, if underweight, health. But, every morning, he searched for the first gray hair among the ashen blond. He'd vowed that when it appeared, he'd quit the Central Correlationists for the sedentary life of a desk scholar.

At the end of the corridor, he paused before the ornate, ten foot-high doors, took a deep breath, and placed his hand on the sensor plate. Yost gritted his teeth at the grinding whir of heavily taxed servos, badly in need of the attention of the very scarce maintenance crews, but slowly the doors swung inward revealing familiar, red velvet shadows.

The well-upholstered hush, soft, reddish shadows and mixed incenses of the Vesting Chamber created a wholly different world from the angular polished-chrome-and-fluorescent sterility of the rest of the Station. Within that chamber, haunted by the distant moaning of thin, dark winds through jagged rocks, Yost always felt he could believe the stories about the Ballatine race-memory being somehow connected with the spirit world or the Beyond where God sat on His throne and Created. The Ballatine reticence to discuss theology could be due to any number of things. Still, it would be nice to know if there really were a Creator.

As he crossed the threshold, allowing the doors to close behind him, Yost felt his post-hypnotic conditioning taking hold and he yielded. Brushing aside the last wisp of mysticism, he checked his assignment card. It read, G-12, Kolitt.

The door closed and Yost moved to the railing in front of him to survey the huge chamber, which was the off-duty home of CC's resident colony of Ballatine. He was on a circular mezzanine, seven levels above the main floor. All the balconies were partitioned into smaller chambers by heavy hangings richly woven in dark-hued patterns. Only the main floor showed hard, reflecting surfaces, and Yost knew, those were merely the roofs of compartments which were as thoroughly hung inside as the balconies. He could see some of the small, spidery humanoids that served the Ballatine on Bellet, the Ballatine homeworld. "Friends-of-one-part" the Ballatine called them, soulless host bodies to provide mobility for the symbionts. It was their placid certainty in recognizing "soul" that had given rise to the rumors about the Ballatine.

Yost had never been in a main-floor compartment, and he knew he never would be. That was where the Ballatine conducted their conjugation and fission rites. Investiture and Divestiture always took place in a balcony chamber. He was on level G, now he needed to find number twelve and pick up his senior partner for this assignment.

He stepped back to the door, looked both ways along the narrow aisle, spotted number two, three, and four and followed along until he found a hanging with a number 12 woven into the abstract design. He pushed the soft velour aside, allowing the tactile sensation to trigger another post-hypnotic command, and entered.

The incense Kolitt had chosen for his tiny, wedge shaped home smelled like sandalwood, fresh air, and eucalyptus. Even without his hypnotic conditioning, the California-born human found it pleasantly relaxing.

And then he saw the Ballatine, ten pounds of amorphous, red- and black-veined, blue-white tissue floating at ease in his nutrient bath of enriched, Bellet seawater.

Yost checked his card against the clipboard hung from the glassite bowl, double-checked the codes, and then clipped the card in place and lay down on the cot. He rolled up his left sleeve and dangled his arm in the water, brushing the Ballatine gently to signal his readiness.

Only the first contact occasioned a twinge of instinctive revulsion...the primeval human reaction to soft, warm, slimy creatures. Then Kolitt commanded the nerves locally and Yost relaxed. The Investiture would take a good twenty minutes, and for the most of that he would be blind, deaf, and dumb, so he let his absent hypnotist talk him into a refreshing nap. Kolitt, like all his kind, would be considerate, but the procedure could still drive an unprotected human insane.

Yost woke to an oddly alien environment that gradually converged on normality. Then the Ballatine spoke silently in his mind, ::Friend-of-two-parts, I greet you. Have I matched sensory inputs?::

Yost nodded. ::Perfectly. You are Kolitt.::

::Correct. And you are Raymond Yost, among other things.::

::Correct. Now. We've many grave matters to discuss.::

::True. And meanwhile, you will make haste to consume calories lest I damage your health. Allow me to check my synapse linkages before we leave?::

::Please do. Control is all yours. Take me to the Commissary.::

Still lying on the cot, Yost felt his individual muscle fibers tensing and relaxing as the symbiont checked his control. Gaining co-ordination, his body rose to its feet and then, suddenly, he blacked out.

He didn't lose consciousness, so he had time to feel true panic before the room swam back into focus. He was seated on the cot. ::What happened?::

::Deepest apologies, Friend-of-two-parts. Slight fibrillation. No damage. It won't happen again.::

Panic allayed for the moment, Yost asked the question that had haunted him since Proken had talked him into this madness. ::Kolitt, do you feel...all right?::

The inward silence lengthened until Yost felt as if Kolitt were gone. ::Kolitt, I apologize. I didn't mean to offend...::

::Yes, Friend-of-two-parts, our pride is sometimes our worst enemy. Yet, if you doubt me, we'd best undertake no mission together. A partnership such as ours can survive only on trust.::

::If you tell me you can do it, I won't doubt.:: Yost considered Ballatine integrity about the only constant in the shifting universe.

After a moment the reply came and Yost was able to read intonation in the silent voice. ::Ray,:: said Kolitt gravely, ::I have at least six months. I've been thoroughly briefed, and I believe we can perform the task set us.::

::Then let's go. We certainly haven't time to waste.::

Kolitt went through his callisthenic routine and then, with increasing smoothness, piloted their body to the Commissary and even displayed unusual talent in feeding themselves. Yost was surprised at such immediate proficiency until he remembered he'd never worked with such a mature Ballatine before.

But Proken had wanted two Seniors for this mission, and he'd wanted the most experienced Ballatine on the staff...namely Kolitt. And Proken usually got exactly what he wanted.

All through the meal they discussed the details of the mission. The Ballatine's skill at the quasi-telepathic form of communication grew steadily until Yost could read nuances of meaning even more clearly than he could human facial expressions.

All during their four-week journey to Harnuit, the technical details held their attention almost exclusively. They went over everything from local language, customs, and values to planetary geography, political history, and economic resources. In short, they approached the field of operations as Correlationists rather than as spies simply because they knew no other method.

They were still discussing their problem as their tiny ship fell toward the Harnuit Spaceport...the one and only spaceport on the planet.

Yost relaxed and let the Ballatine cope with the antiquated, non-human-built landing grid. He watched his fingers flying over the complex board and reflected that, next to women, symbionts were the handiest kind of people to have around. Too bad the two were incompatible. A Ballatine supplied absolute total recall, an enormous encyclopedic knowledge, assorted manual skills, freedom from parasitic invasions, swift repair of injuries, and, most important to travelers, companionship. All at the cost of two or three thousand calories a day...and Ballatines weren't fussy about the original form of those calories.

Yost had become close friends with every partner he'd ever had and now found himself warming to Kolitt in the same way. It was becoming more and more difficult for him to accept the idea of Kolitt's approaching death. Though no further mention had been made of it, it was never far from Yost's thoughts.

When their ship was safely grounded, Yost said silently, ::O.K., where to?::

::It's your turn, I'm going to sleep::

From Kolitt's heavy tone, Yost guessed that the landing had tired his partner so he locked the ship and went to do battle with the local customs authorities. Despite their reputation, spies spent as much time on dreary routine as scholars or anybody else.

Harnuit's largest and capital city, Tobuin, sprawled in rural splendor, practically untouched by galactic civilization. The natives liked it that way, and they didn't welcome tourists.

The terms of Harnuit's Confluence Membership placed an absolute embargo on all Rotsuctronic devices. And practically all modern equipment depended on the ubiquitous Room Temperature Superconductor. What tourist could live even half a day on a strange planet without his personal translator, telepathic shield, and deodorizer? What scholar could operate without his computers and recorders? Unless he was a partner of a Ballatine.

The Harnuiti were spindly-legged, green-skinned humanoids with large, saucer eyes and tiny mouths equipped with double rows of needle-sharp teeth that their thin lips could scarcely cover. Yost knew that, despite appearances, they were not related to anything resembling a Terran frog. Their dental structure indicated a carnivorous ancestry, but they were omnivores. And, like most other humanoids of NCO worlds, they could interbreed with almost any other NCO world's humanoid species...though the results weren't always viable.

Unraveling the hows and whys of the strange, seemingly unnatural phenomenon of interbreeding had been Yost's life work until he took up spying, and so a surge of new energy lifted his feet as he moved out of the spaceport area and into the city.

Every assignment started with the elements of tackling a new planet, learning its languages and cultures, and, finally, moving out among its people to see at first-hand. He always got a thrill out of that first foray into the strange, and it didn't fail him now even though his objectives were different.

With his jump bag balanced on one bony shoulder, Yost bought a couple of the fist-sized, high-caloric

Hardnuts from a street vendor who fished them out of glowing coals and presented them wrapped in fleshy, purple leaves while holding out one knobby, green hand for Yost's wooden coins. Bowing his gratitude, Yost continued down the street, nimbly avoiding piles of dung.

The light held a strange, charcoal-smoke quality that lent colors a glare-free softness very like the first lowering of ominous, black storm clouds. It had a vaguely disturbing effect that hadn't been apparent from the tapes Yost had studied. To allay his nervousness, Yost had to keep reminding himself it was the nearly perpetual half solar eclipse of this latitude that created the effect.

Vaulting the open sewer trough, he crossed the boulevard and entered a likely looking inn whose sign was a faded half circle under which was printed, in native script only, "The Inn of the Half Sun."

The interior was dark and deserted. A lone native drowsed on a high stool in a corner beside a patch of much-bescribbled wall. The untailored length of dingy, gray cloth wound around his emaciated, obviously male frame emphasized his unhuman proportions. But the cloth's relatively clean, new look made it obvious this was the proprietor, desk clerk, and bellboy.

Yost took up a stand at a respectful distance, swung his bag to the straw-strewn floor, and cleared his throat. The sound startled the frail old man and he managed to pry his eyes open. The sight of Yost startled him into a puckered gape that revealed the brown-stained, irregular teeth set loosely in shrunken gums.

The old man said, "Yes? You want something? In the middle of siesta? At high noon, you want something?"

Yost knew the natives slept through the grueling seventy-degree Fahrenheit heat. He said in the local dialect, "I apologize for disturbing you, but I need a room."

The old man peered at the human silently, estimating his worth. He eyed the stuffed Fed bag, then turned to the wall to find a vacancy in his register. "Top floor, west end. Twenty zuit a day."

Yost knew he'd been offered the worst room in the house for twice the price of the best. He had the money, but he dickered the old man down to five a day and breakfast nuts, never letting on that he preferred top-floor corner rooms.

When they'd concluded the deal, Yost hunted about the large empty room that served as a tavern, found the local excuse for a broom, shouldered his bag, and climbed the stairs with a nonchalance that left the old man gaping at the human's enormous strength. That also was calculated. Now, they wouldn't try to roll him.

He found his room, with the lockless door swinging gently in the breeze from the unglazed windows. As he'd expected, it was a long, rectangular room with two inches of reeking, soggy straw on the floor. He swept the straw out into a neat pile in the corridor, propped the broom beside it, and set up camp. It took him twenty minutes to arrange the tent, air mattress, cookstove, and security alarms to his satisfaction.

Then he took his nuts to the window and surveyed the city, absorbing the sinister atmosphere created by the weird lighting.

Presently, his partner joined him. He made no overt sign, but Yost knew another being now shared his eyes. It was a comfortable, secure feeling. As he gnawed the warm, blue nutflesh and savored the smoky taste, Yost said, ::I call a strategy conference.::

::Convened,:: came the silent agreement.

Yost felt the wry smile that went with that. It raised his spirits a bit as he said, ::That caravansary over there::—he focused his eyes on the tallest structure in sight, a dun-colored adobe tower—::looks promising. Hire a native guide, some transport, and set out for Rogahm's studio?::

::Why don't we try the Art Gallery first? That's where the tapestry disappeared from and they're the ones that have been complaining loudest. We're here to find out why, so why not ask? Could save a lot of trouble.::

::That's what I like. A subtle Ballatine. Walk right into a public building and start asking questions that are bound to alert the entire Harnuit underground. The Curiosity Corps could use a couple more like you.:: He gave their agency one of his favorite nicknames in hopes of maintaining his good spirits.

Too late, the stony silence within alerted him to his mistake. Fission inevitably produced two Ballatines. He hadn't meant to imply that Kolitt's children would be unwelcome.

::I'm sorry, Kolitt. I just meant that we think too much like CC data collectors and not enough like spies for this mission.::

Kolitt came back, ::Misunderstanding nullified, Friend-of-two-parts.:: He used the Ballatine idiom for mutual apology. Yost knew it was a formula that erased the whole incident. But, it seemed far more powerful than necessary. And he'd never known a Ballatine to toss that phrase off lightly.

Kolitt continued, ::I don't think the frontal approach is out of order. Asking questions is our profession, so why not ask some?::

::O.K. That's what we'll do, first thing after sundown.:: He fell silent, nibbling at the second nut and at his latest pet worry.

Finally, Kolitt said, ::All right; what's eating you?::

Yost started a flip reply, then swallowed and said seriously, ::Listen, Kolitt, we've chewed this assignment over a hundred times. We've discussed every aspect of it, except one.::

::Go on.::

::The first time you took control, you loused it up. That's never happened to me before.::

::It's never happened to me before either. I thought I explained.::

::No you didn't, not really. It's not that I don't trust you...but if you run out of time, I'm in bad trouble... right?::

::You have a point, Friend-of-two-parts. But, you can count on at least twenty more weeks.::

::What caused that first fumble?::

Silence.

::All right. Here's a worse one. Conjugation?::

The silence clicked off into abandonment.

::Kolitt?::

A few moments later, he replied, ::Here, Friend-of-two-parts.::

::I don't want to embarrass you, Kolitt, but I feel I have a right to know. There practically isn't a race in the whole Confluence that doesn't have strong emotions on such functions. Humans are no exceptions.::

::Ray, I...was on the verge of accepting a...relationship when Proken called me for this assignment. I thought about it very hard, for a long time, and decided it would be best to wait. Do you understand now?::

::Not exactly. I've never had a post-conjugal partner, but I understand there is a difference.::

Kolitt was amused. ::Yes...indeed.::

::What caused that fumble?::

::I was thinking too hard about...someone else. That preoccupation is gone now, so there will be no further difficulty.::

::Except that you're maybe a bit more nervous and sensitive than you used to be?::

The symbiont conceded, ::Maybe.::

::Aren't you afraid?::

::Of what?::

::Dying.::

::No. Dissolution of personality at the proper time and in the proper way is not frightening.::

::It frightens me,:: Yost admitted. Since he'd probed so deeply into Kolitt's privacy, at least he could share his own most private fears. He asked, ::Where does a 'dissolved' personality go? Is death the end? And if it is, does that mean that the whole, frantic churning of life is meaningless? Is there a God to receive our souls? Or does the concept of soul have any reality? Does life have any meaning? Does death have any significance? It won't matter how long I live. Death will always frighten me.::

::I am sorry.::

Yost read true sympathy in that, but also the ever-present refusal of the Ballatine to discuss any aspect of theology. They wouldn't even go so far as to assert that humans, or any other species, need not be frightened. The closest thing to a statement on theology that anyone had ever gotten out of a Ballatine was that friend-of-two-parts appellation. And that was never really explained or discussed either. Yost was not surprised when Kolitt retired for the rest of the afternoon, refusing to engage in any conversation.

As dusk fell and the town lit up with torches, hearth fires, and candles, Yost went in search of the local Art Gallery.

Harnuit's art was not connected with the religions and the Harnuiti didn't decorate everything in sight. They reserved their efforts for items called Tapestries displayed only in public art galleries.

Yost found the capital city's Gallery down a narrow, dingy alley lined with tiny shops that overflowed onto the dung-paved ground. Across the end of the alley, two crude wooden doors opened in an unadorned wall spilling a soft, yellow radiance on the jumbled merchandise.

Entering the flickering shadows, Yost dropped a coin in the metal box chained to a post, and clasped his hands behind his back in the local gesture of concentrated reverence.

The Gallery was a single, large, low-ceilinged room divided into compartments by opaque draperies suspended from the insect-infested rafters. The first compartment opened directly before the door and Yost nodded appreciatively at the way the clean, black draperies focused the attention on the display piece hung across the end of the compartment.

The Tapestry was a rectangle, Yost estimated about six by seven feet, and it consisted of thousands of brightly colored, translucent beads strung on a transparent fiber and woven into a richly detailed, abstract design. By the dancing light that filtered through the Tapestry, Yost distinguished several complementary shapes among the tightly packed beads. At first, he thought he was on the wrong side of the hanging, but then he noticed that the light came from lanterns set in a very narrow space behind the Tapestry and backed by a shiny material.

Stepping back to admire the effect, Yost said silently, ::This looks like something you could appreciate, Kolitt?::

::I shall reserve judgment, Friend-of-two-parts. The

form seems to have possibilities.::

Surprised, the human said, ::Are you an artist?::

::Not really. A connoisseur, perhaps.::

Yost sniffed. ::What's that?::

::What?::

::I smell something. Spice? Incense?::

:There are no new olfactory signals of that description originating in your nasal passages.::

::No? Well. That must be what Proken meant when he said Harnuit's art is quasi-olfactory.::

::I suggest we speak to the proprietor of this establishment.::

::Certainly. How do we find him?::

::Walk about. He'll find us.::

Yost did as he was told, pausing occasionally to examine one or another piece. All of the designs seemed to be abstract and each had its own scent. The proprietor found him as he was enjoying spiced peaches and brandy.

The green skinned, white-robed figure emerged from the shadowy maze to stand half bathed in the eerie, flickering light. He seemed to be of a heavier build than the other natives. In a low-pitched, cultured voice he said, "Welcome. May I be of service?"

Yost sorted himself into the native language and answered, "Perhaps you can answer a few questions for me?"

"Of course. I know every piece in my Gallery."

"There is one in particular I've heard about. The Newsnet Interstellar reviewer called it the 'Vanillamint

Tapestry.' Do you know it?"

"Of course. However, you will not able to view it. It has been stolen."

"No!"

"We have taken the matter to the Interstellar Authorities; however, we despair of ever getting it back."

"Was it that significant? You have so many excellent ones here. What could make any single one that important?"

"Each one is unique. Until its theft, the 'Vanillamint' gave much joy to many of my clients."

"Was it an item of great value?"

"How does one measure the value of the unique?"

"Perhaps the artist could be persuaded to sell me another one like the 'Vanillamint'? Could you tell me where to find him?"

"Tapestries are not sold, sir. However, the creator of the 'Vanillamint' is a novice so I doubt if he has anything else as significant."

"Then how do the artists make a living...if they don't sell their work?"

"Their Hermit Colonies are supported from the public treasury."

"Oh. Then the creator of the 'Vanillamint'...what did you say his name was?"

"Rogahm."

"He lives in a Hermit Colony?"

"Yes, of course."

"And you are the sole agent displaying his work?"

"Yes."

"What else of his is here?"

"Why nothing. I told you, he is a novice. The 'Vanillamint' is the first of his works worthy of display. That is one reason he is so anxious to get it back."

"I thought you owned it?"

"Oh, no. How could it be possible for a work of art not to be owned by its creator? I'm merely his legal representative."

"I see. I'm still curious about the creation of these Tapestries. Would it be possible for me to visit Rogahm's studio?"

"I don't think so. Even I go there very seldom. It was on my last visit that I discovered the 'Vanillamint' just being finished. He's certainly not had time to do anything significant since...and I assure you his previous work is quite worthless."

"If it's that worthless, perhaps he could be persuaded to part with one or two examples. I should like to visit him."

"It would be a difficult trek through perilous and unpleasant desert and, I assure you, quite fruitless."

"I've already come a long way. And it's my time, my discomfort, and my curiosity, sir. If you could give me some clue how to find him, I would be most...generously...grateful." Yost allowed his hand to drift toward a pocket suggestively.

"Well, since you put it that way...I can do even more. I'll arrange for a guide. My own personal servant, Groumain. He's very reliable and a willing worker who can make your journey less unpleasant."

"That kindness will be unnecessary. I'm sure I can find someone...."

"Oh, no trouble. In fact, I insist."

"I couldn't take your servant from you, even for a short time." *And,* he thought, *I could do without your spy.*

"It's no hardship. I have others. Truly, I insist."

They dickered over the price for several minutes and finally agreed that Groumain would assemble transport and camping equipment and meet Yost at the Inn of the Half Sun in two days.

As they walked back to the inn through the teeming, dark streets, Kolitt said, ::I believe Groumain may be an error.::

::What! Subtlety at last? I know he is. But how could I have refused?::

::A good question, but utterly academic. We shall have to keep an eye on this Groumain.::

::You know, we shouldn't get too melodramatic. Central Intelligence is out chasing thousands of clues on an important theft of a something-or-other which we aren't cleared to know about...::

::Which you aren't cleared to know about.::

::Oh? Well. I guess one of us had to know. Anyway, they wouldn't have sent two amateurs on a really hot trail. They're not looking for the Tapestry. It's just that it disappeared coincidentally. So I think we ought to stop seeing spies everywhere and just enjoy ourselves. I don't know about you, but I could use a vacation from chasing will-o'-the-wisp theories about the evolution of intelligent life. A ride through picturesque desert country sounds inviting.::

::Friend-of-two-parts::—Yost recognized the grave tone he'd come to associate with Kolitt's approaching demise—::I'm incapable of enjoying this waste of time. The only reason I'm here at all is that Proken is an unusually persuasive administrator and my ancestors owed him a favor.::

::I know what you mean.:: Yost couldn't count the times he'd been talked into tackling distasteful or dangerous jobs by the "highly persuasive" director. ::And I do hate having to sit here doing nothing for a whole day.::

::So, we'll look up our guide and watch the preparations.::

::Fine idea.::

::But first, another meal and a night's rest.::

::You're determined to put some weight on me, aren't you?::

::Not particularly. I'm more interested in putting some weight on me. But you could certainly use some reserve.::

The next morning found them waiting for Groumain at the caravansary as the smoky light of the half-sun grew slowly into full dawn. Yost stood beside the stone watering trough that occupied the center of the yard and watched the caravansary come to life under the crisp dew of a chill dawn. Discreet questioning of the handlers obtained excellent character references for

Groumain, and when the native guide arrived, Yost was reassured by his appearance as well.

Groumain was taller than most of the locals, well fed, and of a healthy green hue. The length of cloth wound about his torso was a clean black and he had a spring in his step that spelled self-sufficiency. As they watched him organizing transport and supplies, Yost and Kolitt both agreed he was more intelligent, efficient, and dominant than one expected in a slave. He was scrupulously honest in his dealings and the fairness and firmness of his prices were unquestioned.

When he'd rented a corner stall and hired a boy to clean it and care for the rented animals, Groumain came over to Yost, obviously appreciative that the human had not interfered with his work since introducing himself. "Sir, perhaps you could give me some idea of how many maisu will be needed for your baggage?"

Yost eyed the huge, pad-footed, green-haired beasts with broad, flat rumps, bulging sides, and four spindly legs. They were something of a cross between a water buffalo and a camel, but with the vile disposition of a llama. "I believe one will be sufficient for my kit."

"My master has informed me you require three times the food of an ordinary man. This is accurate?"

"Yes."

"Then we'll need two maisu for supplies. It's a long way into the desert. With luck, two talu."

Yost translated. About three weeks. Three weeks out, three weeks back, and four weeks home. Ten weeks and they had only twenty...nineteen and a half.

He said, "Yes, I realize that. I have my own camping equipment, but I'll leave the food and water supplies to your judgment."

Groumain looked around the rapidly emptying caravansary. The watering trough was deserted as the sun now shown weakly on it and the walls surrounding the square stood on their own shadows. The maisu huddled in their ground-floor stables with their attendants, and the caravan travelers, the few who were laying over for the day, had taken to their second-floor rooms, above the thickest of the animal stench. Groumain said, "I'll complete our arrangements this evening and we'll leave in the morning."

Yost nodded. "That will do." Of course, he'd check the "arrangements." He was no stranger to deserts.

The next morning, Yost appeared with his bag on his shoulder, dressed in a crisp, blue traveling coverall, almost before the nut vendors had fired up their coal basins for the day. He insisted on helping the stable boy load the maisu and unobtrusively took inventory. The only problem would be water and everyone he'd spoken to had said there was plenty in the northern desert if you knew where to look.

Yost checked his folding dousing rod, slung it on a chain around his neck, and pocketed his purification kit. They were both legal on Harnuit since they employed nothing more sophisticated than solid-state, integrated circuits and basic chemistry. But some things were best not left for baggage.

When Groumain arrived, they shared a quick meal,

mounted their maisu, and departed with the largest caravan Yost had yet seen assembled at the caravansary.

The lead maisu was carrying a boy and two huge ceramic jars of water with skins stretched across their mouths on which he beat out a rhythm. The sound had a musical boiiioing reverberation that soon had the maisu marching in step, one TWO THREE four...one TWO THREE four...over and over to a chanted tune that seemed the quintessence of movement.

Yost breathed deeply, head high, thoroughly enjoying himself in spite of the dust, ripe dung, chafing crotch, assorted vermin, and depressing lighting. He thrived on strange and colorful experiences, primitive or sophisticated, and he'd certainly been in more miserable circumstances on many occasions, so he was prepared to enjoy an interlude of relative comfort.

They followed the caravan for all of the first week while segments of it split off almost daily to seek their own destinations. Each day the sun became dimmer and they marched longer into the noon hour. Then one day, as the caravan settled down for siesta around an oasis that consisted of an adobe-walled well with hand-drawn bucket, Groumain peeled off to the north.

Now that it was gone, Yost noticed they'd actually been on a trail of sorts. But here the ground was almost virgin. And it wasn't long before Yost felt the lack of a drummer. The four maisu ahead of him now marched in random rhythm and their loads swayed sickeningly.

They marched through the whole day as the gloom

increased toward full eclipse. The sparse desert vegetation became even more scraggly and finally disappeared, leaving the sharp stones with only the wind to grind them to sand. The footing became so bad, the maisu often refused to put weight on one foot or another in a random pattern of jarring limps.

The days passed, and Yost found himself relying more and more on Kolitt to keep his spirits up. Toward the end of the second week, as the watery gloom deepened toward dusk and the lighting seemed particularly oppressive, he said, ::This artist's colony is supposed to be under the exact center of the fully eclipsed part of the continent. How do they stand it?::

::You find the lighting has an emotional impact?::

::Well, doesn't it?::

::Not on me.::

::Why?::

::Because human nerve impulse codes aren't my natural aesthetic referents. Now, if I were using a friend-of-one-part I might be able to judge the effect. But I doubt if their eyes could take this light intensity. So, I'll never see it other than as a partner to a friend-of-two-parts.::

::Do you regret that?::

::No. Working for CC, I go places and see things that I'd never be able to experience otherwise. The price is high. Sharing the body of an intelligent creature, a friend-of-two-parts, rather than being master of a domesticated nonentity that never talks back or vetoes...or fails to eat enough...::

::Was that a gentle hint?:: said Yost, unwrapping a nut as his maisu plodded jerkily behind the others.

::Not so gentle, Ray.:: Yost read burbling laughter of embarrassment. ::I'm starving!::

::So I'm eating. Just be sure this beast doesn't make me motion sick.::

::Have I ever let it do that?::

::No. But there's always a first time.:: Yost would never forget one particular first time...at least, he wouldn't until he'd delivered his partner safely home. ::How are you feeling?::

::As well as can be expected for my age. You have nothing to worry about.::

::Nevertheless, I do worry. What do you mean 'as well as can be expected'?::

::I require more sleep and I'm always hungry. That's all. It shouldn't bother you. Your kidneys are sufficient for the task.::

::You're growing?::

::Spontaneously. An unavoidable necessity.::

Yost remembered the course in Ballatine physiology he'd taken nine years ago. He should have reread the text before this mission, but he'd been so rushed...and it would hardly have been polite after Investiture. ::As I recall, the growth curve is unaffected by conjugation?::

Silence. Total withdrawal. Yost felt a panic of abandonment and was instantly contrite. ::Kolitt?::

::Here, Friend-of-two-parts. Another point...a friend-of-one-part doesn't ask questions.::

::I'm sorry.::

::Partly my fault. Yes. It is unaffected.::

::Then you'll be about double your size by the time we get home.::

::Three quarters.::

::And if we don't make it?::

Silence. The Kolitt seemed to choke on his negation. ::Please...::

Yost prompted, ::It happens anyway, doesn't it?::

Anguish. ::God help me, no, not like that!:: It was the first time Yost had ever known of a Ballatine invoking a deity. The overwash of emotion almost knocked him off the maisu.

::Kolitt, I'm sorry, but it helps to face facts.::

::Friend-of-two-parts, believe me, I'd die first. If necessary, I'll simply leave you. But it won't be necessary. There's plenty of time.::

Yost couldn't help wondering if the Ballatine would be able to commit suicide at such a point in the life cycle. As he recalled, the texts had been vague on the subject. At any rate, he wasn't eager to try Divestiture outside of Chambers and without the protection of hypnotic conditioning.

Yost said thoughtfully, ::Can God help us?::

Silence.

Yost let the subject drop. A slip? Or a figure of speech picked up from a lifetime association with humans? He knew he'd draw no further comment from the Ballatine, so he applied himself to eating the smoky nut and kept a careful eye on his compass. With Kolitt's memory, they should have no trouble finding their way back alone, but he was uncomfortably aware that he might be making the trip in true solitude.

Through the long, dry, but not uncomfortably hot days Groumain was the perfect servant. He was quiet, efficient thoughtful, and industrious. He even made it his business to learn how to set up Yost's tent, and from then on refined his technique until he could make or break camp faster than Yost thought possible. Between a Ballatine and such a servant, Yost often reflected, traveling in primitive fashion was a real pleasure.

Nevertheless, when Groumain announced that the next day would see them at Rogahm's, Yost knew a lightening of spirit that only served to underscore the sense of doom from the watery, charcoal-smoke lighting. He found himself eager to get the job over with and get out of this forsaken land.

They made camp for the night beside one of the typical adobe wells that dotted the trail at two-day intervals and, about midnight, Yost woke to sharp hunger pangs. ::Kolitt? Hungry again?::

::Apologies, Friend-of-two-parts. I'm consuming energy at an increasing rate. I'll calm your stomach. You need your rest.::

::I'm awake now. You must really be starving. I'll just take a walk, eat a nut, and look at the stars. At least the night sky isn't smoky!::

::All right.:: Yost felt Kolitt's embarrassment at allowing his host to feel even slight discomfort. ::But, Friend-of-two-parts, make it two nuts.::

Yost rolled out, thrust two nuts into the glowing

remains of Groumain's fire, and scooted back to the tent for a warm coat against the desert night's chill. Dressed, he skewered his nuts on the slender metal rods Groumain had set out for their breakfast and moved quietly out of camp, lighting his way with a lantern.

::Keep watch, Kolitt, so we don't get lost.::

Presently, he found a nice boulder with a seat-like depression and settled down to munch the warm nut-flesh while admiring the night sky. That was another good thing about traveling with a Ballatine.

No matter what you ate, or how much of it, it always tasted magnificent.

::Ray! Let me!:: Kolitt commanded sharply as he took control of Yost's head and eyes.

Yost relaxed and let the Ballatine focus his gaze, knowing that the symbiont had no peripheral blindness. The streak of light across the northern sky was just fading when he found it. Kolitt said, ::I couldn't tell if it was a meteor or...::

::Or a ship landing?:: supplied Yost. ::There's no spaceport over there...only the Hermit Colony...::

::And Rogahm.::

::Ohhh...bah! This is ridiculous. Send a couple of overly imaginative amateurs to chase...what? What in the universe are we after, anyway?::

Silent chuckle. Then, ::Let's go back to sleep.::

::I'm not sleepy anymore. I'll dream sinister space-ships!::

::You're exhausted. I guarantee you'll be asleep the minute you zip in.::

::All I do all day is sit on that damn maisu. Groumain is the one who fights with the contrary beasts. How come I get so tired?::

::Because I'm working hard! Now move before I do it for you.:: Kolitt's tone reminded Yost of a soft-hearted parent trying to scold a lovable three-year-old.

The Ballatine wasn't that much his senior!

Smiling, Yost replied, climbing to his feet, ::Don't get tough with me, little partner. I'll starve you.::

Kolitt laughed, ::You already are!::

Chuckling, Yost made his way back to his sleeping bag.

The next day, about noon, they topped a final ridge and drew up to survey the Hermit Colony. The watery gloom threw the desert into a tricky, shadowless perspective and Yost found it difficult to estimate the size of the crater that cupped the fifty or so huts of the Colony. The glare-free lighting emphasized the brilliant colors of the stones that lay strewn about the floor of the crater, but somehow the harlequin patchwork of color lacked any trace of high-spirited gaiety. It wouldn't take much to make it sinister as mysterious spaceships.

The garishly bright purples, greens, blues, blacks, and reds were mixed with whites and oranges that seemed to glow in the weird light. There were a dozen shades of scintillating browns and too vivid yellows and hundreds of hues he couldn't name. The effect was so grotesque, he searched for a harmless, commonplace simile. Yes. It looked like a paint laboratory's testing site! He could hardly believe it was natural... and yet, he'd read the reports and knew, intellectually, that it was a work of nature...though it looked more like the work of the devil.

There were no paths between the rectangular, pastel-colored huts that lay widely spaced among the rocks and around the sides of the crater. A single, clean trail led from the rim near them straight across the floor and disappeared halfway up the other side. Yost moved his maisu closer to Groumain's and said, "Which house is Rogahm's?"

The guide pointed a long, green finger. "On the far rim, the pink one."

Kolitt said to Yost, ::If I'm not mistaken, that's on a direct line between our camp last night and the point where the ship landed.::

::Or meteor.:: To Groumain, he said, "Well, let's go."

Silently, the native led off down the sloping side of the crater and struck a brisk pace along the cleared pathway. Soon they were climbing again and before long they'd run out of path and dismounted to lead the maisu the rest of the way up to the rim.

From the top of the ridge, Rogahm's hut commanded a view of the northern desert plain and all its boulder-strewn barrenness. Yost counted a dozen steep ravines within the first mile. If a ship had landed in that...well, it'd probably crashed. And if it had crashed, they'd have heard the explosion. So, it must have been a meteor.

They circled the pink building and found that the northern wall was composed of nearly a hundred small panes of glass, revealing an interior as colorful as the plain it faced. The hut was filled with Tapestries hung on movable wands suspended from tangled rigging that concealed the rafters.

A native emerged from the depths of translucent veils and approached the door warily. He had a lighter green complexion than Yost had yet seen and walked with a pronounced limp, favoring his right leg. His garment was a swirl of grays and whites, and when he got closer, Yost could make out what looked like a solid mass of burn-scar on his torso and upper arms.

When he opened the door, the native ignored Yost and growled tonelessly, "I'm not ready to show. Go home." And he slammed the door.

Groumain said, "Wait here. I'll see what I can do."

He wrestled the door open and disappeared into the sparkling dimness, leaving the flimsy frame to slam lopsidedly shut behind him.

Yost turned to inspect the rocky northern view. The impression of an impending storm was stronger here even though the sky remained clear blue.

Presently, Groumain called Yost in. They found Rogahm covering a large table with an enormous sheet to conceal his unfinished work. Beside the table were large basins filled with the unstrung beads jumbled together without apparent regard for size or color. He grunted, "Well!"

Groumain said, "This is the human I was telling you about."

Rogahm measured Yost's length, mumbling under

his foul breath, "The answer's no. Now go away and leave me alone."

Yost took a deep breath. He thought, *that's why they call it a Hermit Colony.* "I'm really very interested in your work. Can't I just look around? I might find something over which we could come to some kind of agreement."

Yost watched the fire of avarice kindle in those purple eyes and then cool. Rogahm said, "I don't sell my work." He made it sound obscene.

"But you do lend it for hanging where it might be viewed by more people. Your contract with the Gallery is only for Harnuit. And what is worthless to Harnuit eyes may not be worthless offworld. That might be"— he patted his pocket suggestively—"mutually satisfactory."

Rogahm hesitated, then grunted and turned away. "Look! But be quick about it!"

Yost went to the end hanging and began working his way through the close-packed aisles. It was hard to get the total impression of any one piece and he rarely found any quasi-aroma. But, on the whole, he couldn't see any difference between these and the ones in the Gallery.

Kolitt said, ::This one!::

::What about it?::

::I like it. I think. At any rate, I'd like the chance to judge it in more familiar surroundings. If we are to bargain for any of these, let it be this one.::

Yost stood back to scrutinize the piece. As all the

others, the colors were combined by no rules he knew. But, yes, it did seem to have something of the sandal-wood and eucalyptus air that Kolitt favored. ::O.K. It's all the same to me.:: He went in search of Rogahm and found him seated on the floor staring out at the eternal desert.

"I've found something." As Rogahm unfolded his crippled frame and struggled to his feet, Yost looked around. "Where's Groumain?"

"Prospecting."

Yost shrugged. The Gallery certainly had other artists in the colony. He led the way to Kolitt's choice and began the bargaining. He set his offer high enough to spark greed, but low enough not to seem too eager and let himself be jacked up twenty per cent. Then he held firm, refusing to be put off. He'd learned a thing or two from watching Groumain.

Finally, Rogahm grabbed one of the ropes hanging from the overhead pulleys and yanked. The Eucalyptus Tapestry rolled up as it fell to the floor. "So take it and get out of here. And don't come back!"

Rogahm stalked off into the obscuring layers of Tapestries, leaving Yost to gather up his prize.

The Tapestry proved surprisingly light to his offworld muscles, and it took him only about fifteen minutes to lash the roll securely and carry it out to the maisu. Groumain still hadn't appeared, so he tied it to one of the beasts and then stood gazing out at the weird landscape, breathing deeply of the faint breeze. ::Well, partner, you've got your Tapestry. But what else have we got?::

::I'm not sure. Let's take a walk around the building.::

::What for?::

::Come on! I'm in no mood to argue.::

::All right.:: Yost suppressed a little thrill of alarm at his symbiont's shortness. Yost knew no Ballatine would ever force a partner to do his bidding. But, by the same token, Yost was morally obligated not to deny a partner freedom of movement since the Ballatine had no other alternative. But, considering Kolitt's condition, Yost wasn't sure just how far he could trust him if it came to a real clash of wills.

He mooched all around the pink building and then leaned on the side wall again, gloomily examining the northern desert. ::Well?::

::The building is about twenty per cent larger outside than inside.::

::It is?::

::The studio had all the necessary living accommodations. And there were no obvious doors on the back wall. Yet, there is an additional room.::

::Probably storage.::

::Probably. But storage of what, do you think?::

::All I can think about is the sense of doom radiating from that devil's rock garden out there. You know it's stronger here than anywhere farther south?::

::Truthfully, I hadn't noticed. It doesn't affect me. Let's go ask Rogahm about his back room.::

::Do we have to? He's already thrown us out.::

::Friend-of-two-parts. This will undoubtedly be

my last mission...and my last report. I don't want that report to be any less perfect than my previous ones, and an uninvestigated observation leads to an imperfect report. Let's go.::

::All right. But the sooner we get out of this gloomy atmosphere, the happier I'll be.::

He pushed his shoulder away from the wall, dusted the chalky pink dust off his coverall, and picked his way around to the door. There was nobody in sight, so he went in, checked the work area, and then poked among the hangings. He nosed along the back wall of the studio and, near the center, behind several thicknesses of Tapestry and a clutter of dusty art supplies, he found an ordinary-looking door.

::You see, Kolitt, just a storage room...:: He pushed open the door and called, "Rogahm?" before he noticed the strange quality of the light.

It was a steady, white light...a fluorescent. And the room was no Harnuit storage chamber. It was a gleaming, Confluence style, lock-and-key installation. One end was an efficiency apartment. Down the center was a neat, Rotsuctronics work-bench and along the walls were rows of storage cabinets and lockers. Near the workbench, the door of a floor safe stood up on its hinges. Bent over some apparatus on the workbench were Rogahm and...an offworlder!

For twelve heartbeats, Yost stood there staring at the pair while they stared at him. The offworlder appeared to be some mixed breed from the Sirius Cluster. He had blue skin and a bald head, but his eyes were golden, pupil-less orbs set behind two nictitating membranes. His arms looked strong, but his tunic revealed a contoured back as if vestigial wings had grown there. No telling what other odd combinations were hidden under his gray jumpsuit.

Yost found one corner of his mind bemusedly returning to his life-long professional problem. How could it be that so many different planets throughout the galaxy could develop such similar chemistry that such misogynous interbreeding could occur? The man existed...but it didn't take a scholar to guess that he was the many times illegitimate offspring of a long line of careless prostitutes. Anyone with such a build was automatically tagged a criminal in modern society... and very often became criminal because of it.

The mere sight of the Mixie sent chills of horror through Yost. He felt Kolitt's impatience as the Ballatine attempted to take control and retreat. But it was too late.

The offworlder's hand came up, leveling a gun at Yost. The gun, like the man, was a bastard, but he had no doubt of its effectiveness.

One of the Mixie's huge, blue fists jerked an order toward Yost's left, the end of the room he hadn't examined. The cage he saw there left no doubt of the Mixie's status. It was a plain, unfurnished cube about seven feet on a side and closed in front by a transparent energy barricade generated by a unit housed in a bulge on one of the side walls. Sanitary facilities consisted of a hole in the back corner. This type of animal-display cage had been outlawed five years ago. Now, only outlaws had them.

::Kolitt. What do we do?::

::Follow orders, Friend-of-two-parts. This type of hybrid tends to be very strong and proud of it. They love to use their strength against the society that hates them...and you appear to represent that society.::

Yost took a deep breath and glided carefully into the cage. His buttocks had barely cleared the sill when the field snapped on with an ear-tingling sizzle. He turned to watch his captors. Rogahm was still bent over the Rotsuctronics bench, expertly adjusting some apparatus. He looked up to say to the Mixie, "What are you going to do with him?"

"I told you to get rid of him. Now you'll have to take care of him until the boss decides if he can be of any use. Let's finish this up so I can get out of here quick."

While Yost watched, they bent to their work as if nothing had happened. ::Kolitt, what do you suppose they're up to?::

::Quiet. I want to listen.::

The Mixie straightened up, dexterously twirling a long filament onto a spool with thick, blunt fingers. Then Yost saw they'd been duplicating a record fiber.

The Mixie spoke the native language flawlessly. "Now," he said to Rogahm, "if you hadn't let that fat leech talk you out of the Tapestry in the first place, we wouldn't have to go to all this trouble!"

"It wasn't my fault. How was I to know he'd like it? And how was I to know they'd go and steal it right out of a Gallery? If I hadn't let him take it, he'd have known something was phony about this studio."

"Well, somebody sure as hell does. From now on, no more cute tricks with the Tapestries. You take good care of that snoopy character till the boss says what to do with him." He snapped a cover on the filament reel and picked up the duplicate from the bench. "I've go to get moving. Check the..."

Just then there was a clatter as the front door opened and Groumain's voice called, "Rogahm! Have you seen my offworlder?"

Rogahm limped out into the studio calling, "No! Probably wandered off into the desert to get lost. Had three of those up here last twenty-day. Attracts 'em."

Groumain said, "Yeah. Didn't strike me as the type, though."

"Never can tell with these weirdies."

"Won't take long for this guy to starve. Eats three times the rations of an ordinary man and never puts on a bit of padding. Maybe he was sick or something? That doesn't make sense...why would he spend so much time bargaining over a Tapestry and then just wander off?"

"Sick in the head?"

"Could be. Well, I'm not going to lug that worthless thing back with me. Help me bring it in. Maybe you can make something useful out of it. How much did he give you? Our cut..."

The door clattered again. The Mixie stood rock-steady near the bench with his weapon leveled at Yost, as if it could penetrate the energy barrier. It probably could. He didn't feel like experimenting so he stood silently as the outer door clattered again and Groumain called, "See you in twelve twenty-days."

Rogahm came back, letting the door swing to behind him.

The Mixie said, "Well done for a change." He approached the cage, inspecting Yost skeptically. Maintaining the Harnuit dialect, he asked, "Who are you?"

"Raymond Yost."

"Why'd you come here?"

"To get a Tapestry."

"Why?"

"I heard they were interesting. And they are."

"You're a human." It was an accusation and condemnation.

Yost didn't answer. The Mixie made a threatening gesture. "Well!"

"You might say so." He didn't dare admit to being a pure-blooded, Terran-born human.

"Who do you work for?"

"Myself."

"And who else?"

"Just me."

The Mixie chewed his overly prominent lips as he glared at every stitch of Yost's trail-worn blue coverall. "You're no art collector."

"Desert travel does that to one."

"How come you eat so much?"

"The metabolism I was born with demands fuel...just like yours." Yost switched to Confluential Standard for that, but the Mixie didn't even blink one pair of eyelids.

Instead he asked, "You got a Ballatine?"

Levelly, Yost replied, "No." But he owed his steadiness to Kolitt.

The Mixie was silent for several minutes, then he said, "We'll see about that." He turned back to the bench, took one of the two spools, and tossed it into a floor safe. His back muscles bulged impressively as he heaved the plug into place and set the lock. Yost noted bemusedly that it was the same ordinary-type safe he had in his office. If it was good enough for a criminal, it was certainly good enough for CC.

Yost leaned his back against the wall and slid down to sit on the floor. ::What do you think he meant? There's no way he can detect you, is there?::

Yost was shaking so badly, he didn't see the Mixie drawing Rogahm into the studio saying, "Check out front. I've got to get moving. See you in a twenty-day."

After they'd left, the Ballatine answered his partner, ::No, there's no way he can detect me. But...well, Friend-of-two-parts, all the races of the galaxy have those who are for society-as-it-is and those who are against it.::

::You mean there are outlaw Ballatine?::

::I wouldn't put it that way...but that is the effect. The fine points of the Ethic hardly seem pertinent.::

::Kolitt, you're Senior Agent on this mission. How do we get out of this?:: Yost was paralyzed by the thought of an outlaw Ballatine entering his body to do battle with Kolitt. He'd always dismissed such tales as the nightmares of the ignorant. All Ballatine were so damned Ethical. But now, an Ethic of the outlaw?

His partner interrupted his chill thoughts. ::Now that we have what we came for, we are free to return and make our report.::

::Have you cracked up?::

Yost felt Kolitt's laughter before he realized his unfortunate choice of idiom. Fairly bubbling with mirth, the symbiont said, ::Not yet, Friend-of-two-parts, not yet. The successful completion of a mission always has a euphoric effect on me.:: He sobered. ::There is much danger ahead, but we are headed home.::

::You keep saying that, but I don't see it.::

::It's in the Tapestry, Ray. The filament he used to make the Tapestry! It's a recorder fiber. Confluential Intelligence was chasing some information that was on a recorder fiber...the kind of information that can be sold. So we've completed our assignment.::

::But what good's it going to do us, or anybody?::

::It will take time and luck to get out of here...and more, it will take good timing. But I think we can do it. You still have your dousing rod and water kit.::

::You have a plan?::

::A few ideas. It all depends on how well he feeds us, and on what.::

::I don't follow you...but you think we'll have enough time?::

::We'll have enough time if we have enough food.::

They heard the muffled clatter of the front door and presumed the Mixie had just left. ::Call Rogahm and get him to feed us.::

"Rogahm! Rogahm!"

Presently, the artist limped in. "What!"

"Did he leave orders to starve me to death?"

Rogahm looked disgusted and turned back to the studio. "I've got work to do I'll feed you when I get around to it."

"A corpse doesn't eat very well...or answer questions."

The native turned back to his prisoner skeptically and then shuffled to one of the cabinets to wrestle out a case of Service field rations. Cracking it open, he extracted four of the packets and a tube of water. He set them on the sill of the cage and disappeared around the side to push the button. The field extended over the rations and they were sucked into the cage.

Yost said glumly, "Thank you." As the old man shuffled out of the room, Yost picked up his meal. ::T.Y.U.'s,:: he read the labels. ::Will this do you?::

::Yes, Friend-of-two-parts, I believe it will, in sufficient quantity. But only if you eat it.::

Yost bit off the corner of the flexipack, chewed it, and then sucked on the pasty substance that was supposed to be a complete nutrient to his species. It tasted just marvelous, though he knew without the induced appetite it would be hard to choke down. He'd polished off all four of the packets before Kolitt was satisfied.

::Friend-of-two-parts, I'm going to sleep.::

Yost didn't argue. The Ballatine needed his sleep for sorting the memories that he would pass on. So Yost settled down to being bored and lonely...and scared.

The days passed slowly. There were no outside windows, so Yost lost contact with the ebb and flow of the wan sunlight. He didn't regret the loss particularly. He was accustomed to living under lights. And the blue-white fluoros didn't cast billows of doom clouds through his thoughts. But Kolitt became increasingly withdrawn, leaving Yost with nothing to do but feed the fires of his imagination with twigs from the tree of speculation.

If the Mixie came back before he escaped, he might bring another Ballatine. The uncertainty of what that would mean was more chilling than the thought of dying.

But, then again, he might foil their plans by dying in his cage. The quantity of food was not proving adequate to Kolitt's appetite. And, when Rogahm failed to supply the rations, Yost could feel Kolitt's creeping starvation as a drain on every tissue of his body. In spite of the Ballatine's selfless efforts to limit his consumption and ease Yost's discomfort, the hunger became a kind of feverish nightmare heightened by the fetid closeness of the cage's air.

It was during one such bout that Yost sat propped against one featureless wall of his prison, drowning in physical misery. He kept telling himself it was only a matter of lasting out a temporary sentence in hell until Rogahm would feed them.

But then he discovered he'd been panting until his throat was raw and his limbs were twitching spasmodically. This would never do! He projected urgency into his silent call, ::Kolitt! Kolitt!::

But there was only the silence of abandonment. Almost sobbing, he tried again, ::Kolitt! Please!::

::Yes, Friend-of-two-parts.:: The symbiont's tone was quiet and assured.

::Kolitt, can't you do something? You can control my nerves. Why don't you damp my sensitivity to this hunger?::

There was a long silence and then a projection of infinite sadness. ::I'm doing all I can, Friend-of-two-parts. Remember that I, too, suffer in desperation. I share with you only the most minor portion of that. I dare not do more to alleviate your misery for fear I might injure you permanently. The only thing more that I could do would be to leave you.::

That sobered Yost. ::It's not that bad yet Kolitt...is it?::

::I had not judged it to be that serious, Ray. But if you find my presence intolerable despite my best efforts, I have no other recourse.::

::It's not intolerable.:: To himself he thought, damn Ballatine Ethic...to them death was always preferable to risking damage to a host...and you couldn't argue with them. ::I guess I just forgot that it's even worse for you. I'm sorry I mentioned it.::

::You need not be sorry. Partnership implies a claim on attention...even if only to...how do you put it? Oh, yes, to gripe. I understand that this is an activity essential to human mental health.::

::You needn't be so damn snide about it! Ballatine are pretty queer people too, you know.::

::Now it's my turn to be sorry, Friend-of-two-parts. I didn't intend to be derogatory, only to make conversation. I thought it might help break some of the positive feedback of the misery cycle.::

::What? Oh, you mean, take my mind off my problems?::

::I believe I said that.::

::Well, then maybe you'd care to speculate about what the immediate future holds for us?::

::I hope that Rogahm will come to feed us very soon.::

::I hope so, too, but that's not what I meant.::

::I know, Friend-of-two-parts, but I'm curiously reluctant to discuss the grimmer possibilities.::

::Then let's not discuss it. Let's drive right to the heart of the matter. Kolitt, how much time do you have before you must...well, leave me?::

The silence lasted so long Yost was again becoming acutely aware of the throbbing ache of hunger. But finally Kolitt said, ::It's very difficult to say. There are many factors to considered. Starvation has affected severely. I estimate roughly six, perhaps seven weeks.::

::What! That's less than half...!::

::I'm well aware of that, Friend-of two-parts. And it may not be time enough to complete our mission. Therefore, I elect to exercise the prerogative of the

Senior Field Agent and tell you all I know of our mission before I reach the point where I might...misplace...such memories. It's not a great amount of information, but it will have to go into our report.::

::But, Kolitt, if Intelligence didn't clear me...::

The impatience in the symbiont's reply was Yost's first hint of the nerve wracking battle the Ballatine must be fighting. ::They should have cleared you, Ray. I'm not responsible for the idiocies of deskbound spy chasers! Since our lead has turned out to be a hot one you're entitled to know.::

::What I don't know, they can't extract from me.::

::You won't know anything they don't know already, and it won't make any difference if they know that you know. If we don't get away from here before the Mixie comes back...well, that crowd can be counted on to interrogate to destruction.::

Yost had contemplated just such a fate so often that he couldn't work up a new horror. ::O.K. What's the big secret?::

::In a word...Rotsuc deposits. Precise co-ordinates of nineteen deposits on ten planets in the Empty Wedge. All with assay values greater than the richest Confluential deposit.::

Yost whistled. Nineteen deposits of the rarest mineral known to civilization! And all on uninhabited planets, unclaimed by any member of the Confluence. And all rich! It could destroy the economy overnight! Rotsuc would be so cheap that devices based on Room Temperature Superconductions could be made disposable. Without even trying, he could think of three expensively impractical applications that could become common. And...currency values were based on Rotsuc!

Yost asked, ::And that's the information that was on that fiber?::

::Apparently. Unless, of course, they're only involved in some ordinary deal.::

::No wonder Intelligence went chasing off in all directions and even borrowing manpower! Do they know the locations?::

::No. It was the most closely kept secret of a private development company. The theft can't even be announced without pulling the props out of the market.::

::I can see that!::

::Then you can also see that it is essential that one of us get home to file the report.::

::Of course. But I don't see how we're going to make it inside of six weeks. There are no maisu here in the Colony and we'd never make it back on foot.::

::That is true, Friend-of-two-parts. Therefore, we shall have to commandeer transportation.::

::What transportation? Jet-assisted maisu?::

::Our Mixie friend should return next week. Whatever he uses should be suitable.::

::Very nice. And how are we going to talk him out of his own, personal ship?::

::Friend-of-two-parts::—Kolitt was contrite—::I hadn't intended to ask his permission.::

::You mean just...steal...:: Yost realized how ridiculous his reluctance sounded. But then it hit him. ::But, I thought Ballatine didn't steal...?::

::That was your choice of word, Ray. I had intended to commandeer his ship on an official priority and leave Director Proken to straighten out the legalities. That's his specialty and I think he owes us something for our trouble...don't you? We're not leaving the Mixie stranded. He can counter-commandeer our ship and call for his at the pound.::

::Give a philosopher enough paper...! I still call it stealing, but it doesn't bother my conscience. There's only one little problem. The Mixie may object to us leaving his cage.::

::I hadn't intended to ask permission to leave. We're both free citizens and he has no right to detain us.::

::Agreed. I'm all for it. But how are we going to get out?::

::That, Friend-of-two-parts, was the problem I was working on when you called me. I'm certain I have the information that will unlock this cage, but I seem to have misplaced it in my recent...house-cleaning... LISTEN! Isn't that Rogahm coming now?::

Yost perked up...yes! Now he could hear the scuffling limp of the native's distorted gait. With starvation postponed, Yost hoped time might pass a little faster. He laid himself out and pretended to faint when Rogahm came in. Perhaps that would improve the food service.

And it did. It hardly seemed like a whole week later

when Kolitt roused Yost from his reveries. ::Friend-of-two-parts, I think it is time for us to leave.::

::You still haven't told me how you intend to pull off this miracle.::

Silence. Followed by that grave tone that had come to make Yost so nervous lately. ::My apologies, Ray. But I have only just located the memory of the final steps.::

::Well then, let's go! What do we do first?::

::The power pack of your dousing rod will make a fine detonator for our bomb. Get it out and extract the power capsule.::

Yost fished the little cylinder out of his coverall, unfolded it into a Y, and unscrewed the stem. ::I don't get it, what bomb?::

::It was an obscure item one of my ancestors read in a chemical safety journal. Now, get out your purification kit.::

Yost dug the palm-sized sack of gelatin out of his shoulder pocket. ::Before we set off on any escape attempt, I think I'd better...::

::I know. But don't put it down that hole. The T.Y.U. rations have provided us with a unique catalyst which we'll need for our bomb. But first, squeeze half the gelatin out of the packet and drop the dowsing power pack into the space. Then you can use the stem of the dowsing rod to fill the packet with catalyst.::

Yost did as he was told, surprised that the semisolid his bowels produced was nearly odorless and an ashen gray color. The Ballatine must have been up to some subtle tricks. ::Now what?::

::You can locate the cage's generator by tapping along the wall with the dousing rod's V portion. The rod's circuitry will react to the generator's rotating field.::

Yost followed directions and, sure enough, the half-dismantled dousing rod reacted to the generator's fields, giving him a beautiful electric shock that sent him sprawling halfway across the cage. He picked himself up saying, ::And why didn't you warn me?::

::Friend-of-two-parts, even Ballatine make mistakes. Fortunately, this wasn't a serious one. And may I remind you that electric-shock is more uncomfortable for me than for you?::

::Yeah. Well. Let's be more careful. Did you mark the spot?:: It would take a Ballatine to tell one point from another on that featureless, gray wall.

::Of course. Now we'll use the remaining gelatin to attach the bomb to the wall.::

::That gelatin isn't a glue! It won't hold the weight.::

::Mixed with a little dilute uric acid, it makes a fair plaster.::

Working with mounting skepticism, Yost said, ::What's going to set this thing off?::

::When you poke the V portion of the rod into the force-field barrier, the generator will hit the resonating frequency of the power pack.::

::Are you sure it won't hit my resonating frequency first? And, remember, humans aren't explosion-proof. Are you sure this won't kill us?::

::Sure enough to stake all our lives on it.::

Yost thought...*all our lives*...by Kollitt's count that was three...one human and two Ballatine infants. He shut up and worked grimly. The ship would probably ground any minute and they'd have to be gone before Rogahm and that Mixie got back or they'd surely be finished. It should be easy enough to get lost in the night desert, but then how would they find the Mixie's ship in all those rocks...?

The explosion deafened Yost and stunned him almost senseless. But his body was up and moving before the reverberations had died.

Making a supreme effort to collect his wits, Yost wrested control from the Ballatine and dug in his heels. ::Kolitt, wait! What do you know about safecracking?::

::Nothing, Friend-of-two-parts. Let's go! We don't have much time.::

::How much time?::

::Perhaps fifteen minutes. But I can't guarantee that. I'm only guessing he'll cut through the Customs Satellites' midnight blind spot.::

Yost knelt by the floor safe and examined it. Even at close range, it looked just like the one he had in his office...and they had a reputation for being temperamental. Especially when installed horizontally.

::Friend-of-two-parts, the Mixie might have a surveillance-neutralizer on his ship. He could come down at any time.::

::I don't think so. He was in an awful hurry to get out of here. I think he was trying to make rendezvous with a hole in the customs net.:: Now that he was out of the cage, the heady aroma of cool, fresh air was going to his head. He was a man and he was going to act like one. He spun the dials on the safe door and began thumping on the mechanism here and there.

::Ray! If they find us here, they'll surely kill us. The mission...::

::Exactly,:: Yost grunted as he pounded his way around the circular rim of the plug. ::The mission comes first. If that filiament contained Rotsuc locations that Intelligence doesn't have, we've got to bring that information back. If it doesn't, we've got to know because we don't want to send Intelligence on a wild-goose chase that could divert enough manpower to let the real thieves get away.::

::But::—the Ballatine adopted a reasoning tone— ::Friend-of-two-parts, you'll never open a safe with your bare hands. What do you know about safecracking?::

::Very little. But I know something about cracking this safe. I do it all the time.:: He continued pounding the safe in a spiral toward the center. Sweat beaded his brow and he felt faint from the exertion after his long confinement. ::You know how it is around Central. You can never get a repairman when you need one. So, one night, I took the safe repairman out and got him drunk and he taught me how to open these safes without the combination. It works on mine, maybe it'll work here. Give me a few more minutes.::

::I can't give you what I don't have! Ray, let's get out of here while we still can.::

::I thought you weren't afraid of death?::

::This is not the proper time for me to relinquish personality. I thought you were afraid of death under any circumstances.::

::Well, I am.:: He spun the four dials in reverse and began pounding them in sequence.

::Then let's go. To stay here is suicidal!::

::Kolitt, remember it was you who wanted to come poking our nose into Rogahm's back room. You said you didn't want to file a faulty report. If we don't get this tape, it'll not only be a faulty report, it'll be an inconclusive one. At the moment, I'm more afraid of Proken than I am of the Devil!::

After a short silence, Kolitt said, ::I guess I don't understand humans as well as I thought I did.::

::Nor do I understand Ballatines. Is your own personal survival more important than this information?::

::No. Not really.::

::Then kindly stop my hands from shaking! I've got to adjust these dials.::

Kolitt said nothing, but Yost's fingers steadied and his breathing eased. He turned each of the four gently clockwise, past the zero, and back to zero. When the fourth dial registered zero, Yost stood and twisted the handle set flush with the plug's surface. Then he heaved, feeling the Ballatine add to his strength. He'd pay for that drain on vital resources later, but it would be worth it. He got the plug up on its hinges and knelt to rummage in the hole. It held only three fiber reels. He stuffed all three into his pockets and said, ::Let's go. You guide. My night vision is lousy.::

Crouched low, the Ballatine guided them through the dark studio; he snatched up the rolled Tapestry lying near the door and was out into the night heading into the northern wilderness.

Black boulders hulked on all sides and tiny pebbles rolled and crunched underfoot. The stars decorated the moonless sky but shed no light to see by. Yost knew that the Ballatine had placed his own, light-sensitive tissues between the rods and cones of the human retina and could see perfectly now that the yellow sun was gone. Of course, the boulders wouldn't be surrealistic color splashes in the infrared.

Finally, chest heaving, they crouched between two large boulders to watch the clear sky. ::O.K.,:: said Yost, ::Now what?::

::If my time sense isn't too badly warped, our friend is due to ground any second. Watch carefully, we must get the bearing exactly right if we are to pick up our ship before he discovers we've left.::

::We'd make better time without lugging this Tapestry along.::

::Correct. But we may need it. Hang on to it.::

::All right. But I can't imagine what we might need it for!::

::Perhaps that is for the best, Friend-of...THERE!::

Yost's head whipped around to follow the fire-streak to ground and almost before the afterimage had faded from his retina they were moving toward it, weaving through the black shadow of the moonless night but always progressing toward that invisible landing field in spite of countless detours.

Eventually, they crept to the edge of a ravine and looked down the rock-strewn slope to a cleared floor just large enough for the one-man scout that stood silently on its struts. It was an aerodynamically veined, missile-shaped, surface-to-surface scout. The flat expanse of the vest-pocket landing field was illuminated by a circle of glowing panels that cast a soft, green luminescence on the underside of the ship, and provided landing-grid services of a sort. It appeared to be deserted.

::Friend-of-two-parts, I recognize the model and I have the skill to pilot it, but I must retire now to locate all the memories. Do you think you can get us inside?::

::Leave it to me.::

Yost hefted the Tapestry and made his way down the slope, bracing himself against the loneliness that struck as Kolitt withdrew. He watched the ship for a while, circling outside the perimeter, among the boulders, trying to decide if the Mixie was still inside. Finally, he dashed under the ship's landing gear and attacked the hatch. Much to his surprise, it opened to the third standard combination he tried.

He guessed that a professional thief wouldn't rely on fancy locks because he knew how simple they were to open. Suspiciously, Yost climbed into the brightly lit interior, pulled the Tapestry up behind him, and dogged the hatch so it couldn't be opened from outside. Then he prowled the empty compartments with a heart-racing caution until he completed a thorough inspection from drive to pilot's couch.

He seated himself at the controls, secured the webbing, and surveyed the instruments. Very similar to what he knew, but a much older model. Not as many autocircuits.

::Friend-of-two-parts, allow me.::

Yost yielded to the Ballatine and in a neat twelve minutes they were space borne, hyperlight, and headed home. Yost had to admit he couldn't have done as clean a job. Race memory had some advantages. He said, ::That was almost too easy.::

::Ray,:: Kolitt reproached, ::There was nothing at all easy about it. I'm living on nervous energy and if I don't get some nourishment very soon, you are going to have real trouble.::

Yost freed himself and rummaged about the tiny galley. While he prepared a meal, he munched on a few packets of rations and tasted everything that was open. The Mixie wasn't a very imaginative chef, but a hungry Ballatine will make anything taste delicious.

When he'd seated himself before a hot meal, Yost said, ::There's enough here for the four weeks it'll take to get home. Are we going to make it?::

The gravity was back as the Ballatine replied, ::I honestly don't know, Friend-of-two-parts. If I don't make it, you'll deliver our report.::

::There must be something I can do to help!::

::Nothing. Except eat well.::

::If I somehow improvise a nutrient bath....::

::Friend-of-two-parts, I will not allow...that...to happen. Death is preferable. Before I left, I saw my conjugal brother safely through fission, so my duty to my line is discharged. Only my personal survival is at stake, and I do not wish to survive in that manner. Do you understand?::

::Not really. Or maybe I do, I don't know.:: Yost thought about it for a few minutes. For a Ballatine to fission, prematurely and without conjugation, would mean that the children would be the social equivalent of bastards...and they would probably have some sort of handicap...possibly be too weak to survive....Yost remembered that overwash of violent emotion he'd gotten from Kolitt in the desert. If the Ballatine felt so strongly about it, it must be worth a life....::Yes, Kolitt, I think I do understand.::

::Then there is something you can do, Friend-of-two-parts.::

::Yes?::

::Hang the Tapestry in the sleeping quarters and then go to sleep. You're going to be very tired soon.::

This time, Yost wasn't inclined to argue. If his partner could derive some comfort from the Tapestry, the least he could do was to hang the thing.

The minutes mounted to days and the days to weeks. Yost spent a lot of time drowsing or exercising. Kolitt came less and less often to talk and seemed lethargic and mentally disorganized. Cooking was a hobby of Yost's and, with six meals a day to prepare, he kept busy enough. When he wasn't busy, he found himself worrying fruitlessly. There was absolutely nothing he could do.

In an effort to dispel the gloom, Yost took out the fiber reels he'd stolen and played them through the ship's main viewscreen.

The first one was a cryptic list of names and numbers. Possibly a payroll, but to whom? The names were some sort of code.

The second proved to be even less interesting. It contained nothing but binary digits. The computer identified it as a standard route to a local pleasure planet.

But the third! It also was mostly numbers, but even Yost could see that it was a list of co-ordinates for ten planets and longitude and latitude listings for nineteen different sites on those planets!

Using the excitement that discovery generated, he composed their report. He made it completely detailed and scrupulously accurate and, when he'd finished, he took several days to polish it.

Finally, he affixed his signature to the completed document and then called Kolitt.

It took several tries, and when Kolitt finally answered, he was groggy.

::Friend-of-two-parts, you want me to read and sign the report?::

::Yes. At least that gets the formalities out of our hair.::

There was a long pause as if the symbiont were laboring to think clearly, then he said, ::I'm afraid my signature would be quite meaningless at this point. I trust you....::

::Meaningless? Why?::

::I'm...::—another long, labored pause, then sharply—::Ray, go lie down on the bed.::

::What? I just got up! It's almost time to eat.::

The Ballatine's reply was faint and, Yost thought, a bit ragged. ::Don't argue! Go! I haven't got....:: Yost felt Kolitt's mental gasp. Something was very wrong!

Yost climbed to his feet and moved gingerly to the sleeping compartment as if afraid that a sudden jar would dislodge a delicately poised disaster.

He lay down on his back and said. ::There. Is that better, Kolitt?::

::Look at the Tapestry.::

Turning his head, Yost examined the hanging. At Kolitt's request, he'd hung it in front of a glow panel so that something of the Gallery's backlighting effect helped bring out the sandalwood and eucalyptus aura. The glistening beadwork was all swirling color and sparkling fire. The shades were dark, mostly reds and browns, but with black and gray patches worked into an optical illusion of three dimensions. Almost. Yost could see why Kolitt liked it. It did remind one strongly of Kolitt's Vesting Chamber. Then, Yost felt the familiar soothing relaxation taking hold. He shook himself and blinked hard at the ceiling.

::No! Friend-of-two-parts, look at the Tapestry!::

::I can't. It's too good. It can even trigger my hypnotic conditioning.::

::I know. That's why we brought it along. Ray, please don't make this any harder than it has to be.::

Suddenly suspicious, Yost said, ::Make what harder?::

Kolitt said in throbbing sadness overlaid with determination, ::I must...leave you, Ray. You've been a good partner, and I dare not risk staying with you longer.::

::No! Kolitt, what's the matter? I thought you had another two weeks at least?::

::I'm not sure, Friend-of-two-parts. My judgment is slipping badly. I almost caused an injury to your brain just now. It was only luck that saved you. I'm becoming clumsy, awkward, and dangerous. I sense already the beginnings of disintegration. I can't tell if there are hours or days yet remaining, but I can't risk damaging you. Now, will you look at the Tapestry and try to let yourself relax? It will all be over very quickly.::

::No! Kolitt, look. You estimated four weeks ago that you had six, maybe seven weeks. We've been eating pretty well lately. Maybe you don't feel well, but you said yourself you can't trust your judgment. Why not trust your original estimate? We'll be home in a few days with a whole week to spare. Hang on a little longer. Take it one day at a time. I'm sure you can make it.::

Kolitt lectured tightly, ::Now that food is plentiful, the starvation-stimulated growth is accelerating. I cannot tell by exactly how much, nor can I predict the exact moment when I must leave you before I lose the power to do so. Divestiture is not simple, Friend-of-two-parts. My purpose would not be served if you were to die as a result of my clumsiness.::

::Kolitt, we've beaten the odds fantastically so far. We're riding a streak of luck. I know it won't run out on us now. How terribly final and irrevocable is death.::

Very quietly, the Ballatine said, ::That is also true for you, Ray. You've told me how much you fear that ultimate end. I can't ask you to face that...or worse, life imprisoned in a useless body.::

::It won't come to that.::

::Which of us is in the better position to judge?::

::You just admitted that your judgment is faulty right now. But mine is the same as ever. And I say, don't panic. Wait. Life is a treasure that cannot be replaced. Fight for it!::

::Your fear of death renders your judgment faulty, Friend-of-two-parts. You fear it so much you're unable to believe that it can happen to you. That is a typical human trait, I understand. It allows you to take illogical risks in the face of danger. You demonstrated that you have that blindness in full measure when you stayed to open the Mixie's safe.::

Yost suppressed a thrill of triumph. He'd succeeded in drawing the Ballatine into conversation. Argument was the Ballatine racial weakness! ::I was right, wasn't I? I did get the thing open, and the tape was of the Rotsuc deposits and we did get away.::

::That, Friend-of-two-parts, is utterly irrelevant. The probability of success was unacceptably low.::

::I can see you're no gambler!::

::Very true. And I do not propose to gamble with your life.::

Damn! Yost thought hard, then he said, ::But it's my life, and my right to gamble with it. What have you got to lose? Maybe you don't fear death, but some ways of dying are preferable to others.::

::Also true. But you do fear death.....::

::But death is the inevitable destiny of all life. I must face it one day. Haven't I the right to choose my own way of dying? Would you rob me of the right to find the circumstances which would give my death meaning and give me the courage to face that ultimate fear?::

::You surprise me, Friend-of-two-parts. I had no idea the average human could plumb such depths of the Ethic.::

Yost didn't object to being called "average." He knew the Ballatine was comparing him to the great human philosophers from the Sirian Totarch clear back to Aristotle. He said, ::But that doesn't answer my question. Do you have the right to rob me of choice?::

Very slowly, as if deliberating each word, Kolitt said, ::It is not who robs you of right. In this case, you are assuming a right which the Ethic does not grant you.::

::But I'm human. I don't live by the Ethic.::

::You have labeled yourself an agnostic and you speak like a philosopher, yet you claim not to subscribe to the Ethic. Then, from what do you derive your morals? Have you considered what would happen if it were known that a Ballatine had caused the death or injury of a friend-of-two-parts? On what grounds do you claim the right to take that risk?::

Yost had to admit that Kolitt had him there. If the ship parked itself in orbit over Central and his body were discovered, a thorough autopsy would be mandatory. They'd certainly discover the cause of death. The Ballatines' relationship with every other intelligent species was based on absolute trust. One incident, no matter how voluntary, would destroy their usefulness as partners and put a serious dent in Central's resources. It might even destroy the stability of the Confluence. Being so huge and diverse, the Confluence was a rickety political structure at best. Deprived of partners, could Central's Agents hold it together at all? Yost didn't know.

But, somehow, deep inside, he knew that if something were right for society, but wrong for the individual, it could not possibly be the correct course. And wasn't that a moral judgment?

He started talking, not quite sure what he was going to say. ::You subscribe to a system called the Ethic which focuses on relating the individual to society. The good of society is the ultimate goal, and all actions and beliefs of the individual must be structured to that goal. Ballatine society bases its morals on the Ethic.

::Such systems were not unknown to human philosophers. I think most humans consider such ideas as lofty goals full of praiseworthy idealism. They consider the Ethic a standard of excellence. But I don't know any humans who actually live by such principles, and I don't know anyone who loses any sleep over their failings.

::The people I've grown up with gave me my morals. You see, Ballatines derive their morals from the Ethic. But humans seem to do it, at least in practice, the other way around. We derive our ethics from our morals.

::But where did our morals come from? The segment of human society from which I come has a moral system based on an ancient, monotheistic religion.

::I've never considered myself a member of any religion. But I've accepted the morals of the religions most prevalent in my environment. All those religions are basically designed to help man deal with the racial fear of death. We all have a great emotional need to know what lies on the other side of the black curtain. You're right, Kolitt, we can't really conceive of personal... dissolution. I suppose that looks pathologically egotistical to you. And maybe it is. But so is our morals system. Our religion is focused on the relation of a man to himself and to God...not to society. We're more interested in guiding the individual to 'right' action so that, ultimately, he can stand in front of his maker with pride.

::I think, Kolitt, that I'm intellectually an agnostic, but emotionally, where it really counts, when it comes to actually making a moral judgment, I do believe in a Creator. And I can't believe that the Creator would want a man to do wrong just to continue a social order. I don't know where that belief comes from. It may be irrational, illogical, and un-Ethical, but nevertheless it is my firm conviction and I can't go against it.

::I suppose, if there is no Creator...no God...then the whole fabric of morals by which I've lived simply disintegrates. But I don't know...I have no way of knowing...if God exists or is merely the figment of our imagination. I don't have the intellectual faith of a religious person to sustain me, therefore I have the right to face death in whatever way seems meaningful to me. I choose to risk my life to save a life. Such risks are considered morally 'right' among humans. Can you convince me that God does not exist? That our moral system is completely wrong?::

There was a long pause, but Yost didn't sense the total withdrawal he'd expected. Finally, Kolitt said, ::Does your morals system give you the right to impose your values on another who does not subscribe to the same system?::

Without hesitating, Yost said, ::Yes, I'm afraid it does, Kolitt. I told you our morals were based on religion...and it's a proselytizing religion. Most humans would deny it these days, but when the chips are down, we really believe we have the one and only 'right.' But in a way, you really do share our values. You don't want to die...like this. I'm not trying to 'save' you from the proper death you seek. The only way you could convince me that I'm wrong is to prove to my emotions that God doesn't exist.::

The long silence showed that he'd made the Ballatine really think. Eventually Kolitt said, ::You refuse to co-operate with Divestiture unless I can prove God doesn't exist?::

::I believe I said that.::

::If I attempt to leave without cooperation, your sanity would certainly be forfeit. I think that if I insist, you will co-operate.::

::Does the Ethic allow you to take that risk?::

::No. But neither does it allow me to remain with you.::

::So, we're both reduced to a choice between evils. A very sticky moral choice. Shall we adjourn to the galley while you think about it?::

::You've made up your mind?::

::Yes. Apparently, I have.::

::I fear that no Ballatine will ever understand human psychology. You realize, of course, that if I leave without your co-operation, and you are rendered insane, it's the same as if I didn't leave and you die.::

::Yes. I have you over a barrel.::

::A very colorful image but somewhat inaccurate.::

When Kolitt's silence lengthened, Yost got up and went in search of a meal. What he was doing scared him more than all his imagined tortures at the hands of the Mixie. He hadn't planned on it. It had just happened. It was another one of those things a man just had to do, scared or not.

Again, the days began to pass, but ever more slowly. Yost spent many hours alternately arguing with and encouraging the Ballatine. He used ever trick of Ballatine psychology he'd ever heard of and even invented a few new ones. He knew that if Kolitt hadn't been suffering from disorganization he'd never have held off even six hours, but six days later, the planetfall alarm went off.

Yost was resting at the time and the Ballatine was in a long period of total withdrawal. Yost clambered up to the control room and threw himself into the pilot's couch. ::Kolitt!! Wake up, partner, we're home!::

::What?::

::Home. Where the devil did they hide the radio...? We can't sit up here in orbit and wait for the tugs!::

::Ohhh...:: Yost felt that groan as if Kolitt was pulling himself out of a feverish slumber by main force of will. ::Let me.::

::You all right?::

::No!:: the Ballatine snapped, ::I'm not all right, and haven't been for days! I only hope I can still pilot this thing. Let me!::

::All yours.::

Yost watched his hands fly as Kolitt worked the radio, got Ballatine Central, and rattled off a command in his own language, ignoring the painful stretching of Yost's throat. The speaker snapped a crisp reply as Kolitt guided the ship down into the emergency berth near the gleaming, gold Ballatine dome nestled among the towers of the sprawling CC complex.

As soon as they had touched down, Kolitt threw the lock seals to "open" and relinquished control of their body with a sluggishness that scared Yost. ::Friend-of-two-parts, go down to the lock...someone will meet you. Do as he says. Hurry.::

Yost moved. As he approached the lock, a friend-of-one-part, undoubtedly guided by a Ballatine, beckoned him urgently to follow. They descended three levels and then hit a large, main corridor lined with plush hangings vague in the dim, red light. The three-foot-tall anthropoid friend-of-one-part sped along, never looking back. Yost stumbled and nearly fell as a strange sensation twisted his guts. Kolitt said, ::Hurry, Ray. It has begun. There are at most only minutes left before I can no longer accept...::

Suddenly, they came to a large, ornate door that flew open at the Ballatine's touch and they were on the main floor of the Vesting Chamber. His guide scampered between the room-sized cubicles and finally opened one of the doors.

Beckoning Yost on, the Ballatine disappeared into the dim interior. Yost entered and stood surveying the fission chamber, wondering what to do. It was well upholstered and richly hung with soft velveteen and was very dim even by Ballatine standards. In the center of the carpeted floor was a pool of crystalline fluid lit from below by a dim, red light. Yost could see the silhouette of a very large, amorphous Ballatine writhing strangely in the fluid nutrient. He'd never seen a Ballatine undulate like that.

"Hurry!" said the guide, "Lie down beside the pool... here."

Confused, Yost stood dumbly, unable to relate to the scene before him. The friend-of-one-part took his arm and guided him gently into place, draping his arm deep into the warm, syrupy liquid where it was promptly engulfed by the gooey softness of flaccid, Ballatine flesh.

Within him, a crawling, creeping, seeping withdrawal made him choke on a scream. He struggled to rise, but the Ballatine friend-of-one-part was holding him down.

Then he knew what was wrong. The unusual entryway hadn't triggered his conditioning! No velvet mystery, no velour hangings, no incense! He said, "My...." He couldn't control his throat.

He tried again, "I...." He gagged!

The friend-of-one-part placed a hot, calloused hand on Yost's forehead, fingers gentle but firm. "Easy, Mr. Yost, Kolitt doesn't have much time. Relax. Fix your eyes on the ceiling and relax." The Ballatine's voice droned on, a deep crooning that blended with his hypnotherapist's tones. Gradually, he found himself letting go, falling into the limbo of complete trust. But it was different. He didn't go completely under. He could still feel the weird symphony of sensations, but it no longer sent him into a panic.

The crawling continued for an eternity. He heard himself whimper as he lost visual and auditory contact. And then, gradually, his senses cleared and there was only one thread of contact left. Dizzy, he almost surrendered consciousness before he heard Kolitt say, ::Thank you, Friend-of-two-parts, and good-bye. There is no way to disprove that which is. God does exist.::

Yost succumbed to oblivion. And when he swam up to consciousness again, he wasn't sure if he'd heard that last. Had he imagined it? But, if not, what did it mean?

He propped himself up on one elbow and looked into the pool. Four red- and black-veined Ballatine floated quietly in the crystal fluid. Two were smaller than the other pair, but they seemed alive and well.

Yost said, wiping a tear off the corner of his eye, ::Thank you, Friend-of-two-parts.::

SCIENCE IS MAGIC SPELLED BACKWARDS

"Mavrana," said my mother impatiently, "just give me one good reason why you won't join the coven!"

"Mama, are you trying to tell me I got my doctorate in nuclear plant management just because your—your—your *coven* performed certain, stupid rituals?!"

"You don't suppose the good citizens of *this* town would have allowed that plant to be built here—just so you could have a job near home—*without* a little encouragement from us?!"

I jibbered and stuttered to a pressed silence. Her idea of scientific evidence had pushed my temper to the flash point and I had to get out of there before my brain melted down.

I stood and dumped my napkin into my soup bowl. "Mama, we're just talking past each other. I'll see you tomorrow."

Quickly, I whirled out of the kitchen, picking up my suitcase from where I had left it by the front door, and made for my car. Blinking away tears, I drove off without considering a destination. Homecoming, after eight years of university hopping, had not turned out as

I'd dreamed it would. What to do now?

I had to report for work tomorrow morning, bright and cheerful and ready to take over the responsibility for the safety systems computer at the Sterling Bridge Nuclear Cycle Plant. It was a big chance for a new Ph.D. I knew I'd earned it. I knew I was ready. But I couldn't do it if I reported in with a crying jag hangover.

I found myself driving by the plant, located in what had been cow pasture and apple orchard when I was in high school. The humped buildings and thrusting towers silhouetted against the sunset sky took my breath away. My spirits lifted and I began to think again.

At the stoplight, I turned onto the new six-lane highway into town. The old town center was coughing itself clear of homebound traffic and rolling up the sidewalks.

I turned onto the two-lane street that had been the entire commercial district when I was a kid, before the shopping malls. The one- and two-story buildings looked tumbledown and dingy to my adult eyes, but I remembered the turns that put me into the parking lot of the Hotel Saginaw.

The clerks were all new. They didn't recognize me, or my name, when I checked in. Room 333. Third floor. That would have meant something profound to Mama, I'm sure.

I fidgeted around the single-bedded, bare room. It was no Lasergloss Inn. I thought of going to a movie, a bar—anything. Instead I took a bath—the plumbing rattled—and went to bed. But I couldn't sleep. No way I could banish my mother's face from my mind's eye. It was just like my freshman year in college all over again.

I flipped on the failing, old television screen, promptly flicked it off, and instead counted the money in my wallet. What was I going to do? I'd counted on living at home, but that was obviously out of the question. Mama wasn't going to let me rest until I joined her group of whackos. I'd have to get an apartment. My salary would cover it—easily—but it would be a month until I got paid.

In all fairness, it did occur to me to wonder how, it was that I'd been offered this marvelous job when the ink on my diploma wasn't even dry yet. *And,* of the ninety-two companies I'd applied to, this one, in my home town, was the only offer I'd gotten. Statistically, it was rather odd. Everyone else in the top ten of my class had gotten dozens of offers.

I lay awake the rest of the night, cataloguing all the lucky breaks I'd had for the last eight years—statistical anomalies all. And now I was boxed into a job which ought to have gone to someone with at least two years' experience. Oh, I was well prepared for it, but *they* didn't know that. So why was I hired?

I watched the dawn, and then grabbed a take-out breakfast and ate on the way to the plant, keyed up as if for a final exam.

The personnel manager met me in the outer office, and before I could catch my breath, I'd been assigned an office, one quarter of a secretary, a security chip that opened some doors, and a whole list of things, I was sitting at my absolutely bare and empty desk staring at a digital photo of the plant that was the only decoration on the white walls, when a man walked in wearing a tag that said he was Alfred McCree.

He was about my own height, with medium brown hair, black eyes, a lovely straight nose, in a face which I estimated at perhaps thirty years old, and he *wasn't* wearing a wedding ring. The smile was dazzling, too. "Ms. Samchik? I'm supposed to train you for the hot seat—that's what we call your job around here."

"That's nice," I said as the room receded into a blur and he emerged with the blinding clarity of a brilliant vector graphic. "I mean," I said shaking myself, "I hadn't known I'd get any more training than a manual to read."

He shrugged. "This plant is so new the manuals haven't been written yet! We went on-line just last year."

I liked his voice, too. "I know."

"But we have a new computer that's going to make this plant the safest in the country—maybe the world. And it's all yours from now own—on one shift anyway. Come I'll show you!"

I followed him across the hall and learned that he had been in the hot seat when the plant opened, and now had been promoted. Within the hour, we had littered the desk, chairs and most of the floors with opened binders, books, and magazines. Every screen in the room displayed one reference or another. Lunch was a cup of coffee, and an hour past quitting time I called a halt when I discovered I couldn't focus my eyes because of the hunger headache lurking behind them.

"Can I drive you home?" he asked.

I remembered how his masculinity had affected me when he'd first walked in. The effect had faded while we were working, but it was coming back. *Well,* I thought with a sigh, *it really isn't good to get too personal with your boss.* I shook my head. "I have my car."

"Can I offer you a dinner to make up for keeping you so late?

I thought fast. The offer was so tempting, considering my flat wallet, but I said, "No, thank you very much. I've got a lot to do—getting settled and all. I'll see you tomorrow." I couldn't afford to let him get the wrong idea about me.

That first month flashed by. I looked up my High School best friend's mother and rented a basement apartment in her house—on credit—and began to set up housekeeping.

Mother insisted on feeding me dinners, and for that I could tolerate her lectures about how the energy problem was still an ongoing worldwide crisis, due to an imbalance in psychic forces, which her coven was working to rebalance. She really believed that the commercial development of clean burning nuclear fusion plants was due to the efforts of the hundreds of groups like hers, and therefore I should want to help them and join her coven.

"Mavrana, this work, is vital. We've already got the world convinced that fusion is as safe as any other energy source. If we don't convince the other half soon, there'll be another depression like there was in the early years of this century. With your magical talent, *why* won't you help us?"

"Mama, why, won't you listen when I tell you there is no way—no way at all—that your prancing and dancing could have altered people's ideas!"

"What do I have to do," she protested, "trigger an earthquake under Sterling Bridge, before you'll admit the obvious?"

"Oh, don't be ridiculous!" I shouted and stormed out.

But I kept coming back—because I liked to eat, and because she did shut up and listen quite often. I had nobody else to burble to about all the wonderful new toys I had to play with, and I wanted to share my success with her. I think I secretly felt that I might even convince her that science works—and magic doesn't. I owed her that much. She was, after all, my mother.

The second month, I worked on the simulator, drilling on every emergency in the book and half a dozen I was inspired to invent. I even presented the earthquake scenario mother had suggested, and though the administrative board thought it far-fetched, they encouraged me to set up procedures.

The third month, I was put to work for real. The hot bed as they affectionately termed the computer room where we controlled the safety systems, had one glass wall overlooking the pit where the main reactor lived. The other wall held the screens monitoring the rest of the plant. It took a crew of eleven to staff it, in four shifts, round the clock.

For the first two weeks, I was never left alone in the hot seat. Randomly they hit me with every exotic drill they could imagine. But I never muffed it, and gradually I stopped worrying about whether it was a drill or real.

Then, one afternoon, McCree met me at shift change, and shook hands solemnly. "You're on your own, Ms. Samchik."

I had never known the meaning of pride before in my life. I wanted to scream for joy. Instead, I took a deep breath and ordered all stations to report. Ten all-clears snapped back to me, clean and crisp as could be. I was in charge of the whole fusion cycle plant.

For weeks it was all fresh and new, important and beautiful. I could sit in the hot seat, surrounded by my own controls and gaze out that majestic window at the pit, and know I'd achieved everything I envisioned as a kid.

But then I began thinking about McCree's new job. He was in charge of acquiring new computers for the plant, and he got to travel all over the world, keeping abreast of research in the field. Six months I'd been out of school, and I could feel my skills becoming outmoded. I began to drop into McCree's office, just to see what he was doing. But he took it for a personal interest.

"I've got two tickets to a Ravens concert for Friday night. Shame to let them go to waste...."

The Ravens had given me my first glimpse of the romanticism behind nuclear fusion—humans harnessing a piece of the sun—and often during difficult exam periods, their recordings had shored up my determination. But *I* hadn't been able to get a ticket to their concert. I gritted my teeth and said, "Fine. I'll take you out to dinner beforehand, okay?"

I *wish* I'd remembered I'd told my mother I wanted a ticket to this concert, and that I'd also mentioned McCree.

At the concert hall, I found he had front center balcony seats. The Ravens came on in feathered black capes and Native American style bird masks which they tossed aside to sing their own songs in the soft, lyrical style they'd made famous.

Their final number was the one that had been their first hit and reprised all the superstitions about the raven, and about how useful their mischief could be when they'd been tamed and trained, ending, "So we'll fly to the sun and bring it down to you." Hearing that in person for the first time, I cried.

As we put on our coats, I said, "I'd really love to meet one of them, but the crowd backstage will be awful."

"I'm game if you are."

Our eyes met and we nodded. But as we inched up the aisle, I saw my mother, with all of those I suspected belonged to the coven, seated in a block just above us. I maneuvered McCree's back to them and tried to hide both of us in the crowd. I don't know why. I'm sure Mama had been watching us the whole evening.

This new theatre had been designed to let crowds flow through backstage in neat autographing funnels. We joined the end of the line and waited. As the line began to move, McCree suddenly said, "I haven't got anything for them to autograph!"

"Neither have I!" We hadn't bought programs, and I'd lost the giveaway ad book in the ladies room. I searched my tiny formal handbag, came up with my wallet and a brainstorm. "I'll have them sign the back of my Plant ID card!" I pried it out of the holder.

He dug his out of an inside pocket. "It'll be worth a million some day!"

As the line crept forward, I began to feel foolish. What, I really wanted was to *meet* these men, not this.

No, what I really want is for them to meet me!

Now that was an embarrassingly adolescent emotion.

When we got to the head of the line, the five Ravens were standing wrapped in black bathrobes, patiently autographing and smiling for pictures. I handed over my card mumbling about it being all I had with me to write on.

Phil Raven turned it over, saying, "What's this? Sterling Bridge Nuclear Cycle Plant? Hey, Art, come here!" The Raven on the end came around, looked at the pass, smiled and handed it back to Phil.

Meanwhile, McCree had handed his card to Dan Raven who was also examining it. Dan, said, "Look, could you two step out around here for a few minutes?

We'd like to talk to you."

Oh, God!

McCree's eyebrow was climbing, but he said amiably, "Sure, I think we have some time."

We were drawn into the dressing room behind them. It was a large suite with a sitting room from which eight small dressing rooms opened.

Soon, their manager cut off the flow of people and herded the five of them into the sitting room, pushing the door shut behind them. "You guys get dressed before you all catch cold!" he shouted at them waving them out of the room.

"But," protested Phil who seemed about to approach us.

The manager came over, waving his cell phone, "Get! Now!"

Phil said at us, "Five minutes, don't move!" and let himself be crowded into one of the dressing rooms. The room's phones began ringing. Someone came in with a fistful of telegrams and a huge flower arrangement. Then several reporters were ushered in. In all, we waited an hour and a half while after-show business ceremonials were dispensed with, but finally Phil, Dan, and Art pulled us into one of the side rooms.

"I've always admired you people who could actually understand all that math. Science has always defeated me," said Dan. "I try to make up for it by writing songs that inspire kids to work hard at learning it."

"It worked," I said, and told them about struggling through college on their inspiration.

"Well, now's a good time to pay the debt. Settle a bet for us, will you?"

I nodded, and Art said, "Ten percent of this grid's power comes from fusion, right? But Sterling Bridge is a fission plant."

Phil said, in that velvet bass voice I loved, "No, I remember distinctly when it was built. It's a fusion plant supplying thirty percent of this grid's power."

"No, that's the grid north of here!" protested Dan.

Art started to say something but McCree cut him off with a raised hand. "Sterling Bridge is the most advanced fusion plant on line now, but the grid has ten percent tidal, eight percent solar, sixty-five percent fission, and seventeen percent fusion, with Sterling Bridge providing half of that. That's approximately. There's still a coal plant on line that can use natural gas in a pinch, and some home owners are selling-back from windmills."

"And you're right, Dan," I added, "the grid north of here has a fusion plant supplying thirty percent of its power."

That settled the bet with no winners and no losers. They all laughed, and as I basked in the amiability of the three stars, I began to understand where their music came from. It only made me more hungry for their company, but now it was time to leave.

McCree's car was the last in the lot, but traffic was still clogging the intersections. We'd seen the Ravens piling into their long, black, chauffeured limousine, still pursued by avid fans. They'd driven away in a different direction, so it was with some surprise that I heard Phil's velvet bass tones coming from a taxi sitting next to us at the traffic light. "I wonder how many of those fans are still following the limo?"

"Get your beak out of my ribs," complained Gordon, one of the Ravens we hadn't actually met.

"That's my elbow, dodo!" answered Art, laughing.

As the cars began to move, I stuck my head out of the window—McCree was driving. It was a very beat-up old taxi. Hardly where you'd expect to find *stars*. On a totally wild impulse, I called, "Mr. Raven?"

Two pale faces appeared at the taxi window. "Oh, what a relief!" To the others, Phil said, "It's not fans." And to me again, he said, "Is the traffic always this bad on the airport road?"

"No, just when the theatre lets out. Are you trying to catch a plane?"

"No, we're staying over."

I had a marvelous idea. "If you'll be here tomorrow, come on out to the plant and we'll see you get the grand tour."

There was a hasty conference as the lines of cars began to separate, and he replied, "Would two o'clock be okay?"

"Fine," I shouted back, overjoyed.

"Look," Phil called over, "we're having some friends in for supper. Follow us, if you have time." And then he was out of range.

That night may go down as the high point of my life. The Ravens never sought us out, but they gave the impression to everyone else there that obviously we belonged. My one penetrating memory was of sitting on the floor with about ten others, listening to Phil and Dan reminiscing about the long string of miraculous breaks over the last twenty years—especially since their comeback some six years ago.

Some of the scrapes they'd been through were hysterically funny, and some were just plain spooky, at least to the daughter of a witch. Others might not be so sensitive to the possibility of a supernatural explanation.

When we left, the Ravens all waved to us, saying, "See you tomorrow!"

In the car, I shook off the star shock and said, "Alfred, do you have any idea what the odds were against this evening happening?"

"That's the first time you've called me Alfred."

"Yeah, but I'd really like to know what the odds were."

"I'll run it up for you tomorrow. Look, it happened, so it wasn't impossible."

But I couldn't help thinking about the hundreds of other Sterling Bridge employees who had been there and would have given anything for the evening we'd had. "If I hadn't lost my program, I wouldn't have thought of them signing the cards."

"So maybe you're psychic and knew about their bet?"

"You don't believe in ESP, do you?"

"I don't *believe* in it, but there *is* something about

living things that sometimes affects random chance, somehow, and bends it to our will. That's been experimentally established."

That was true, but I'd never believed those experiments.

I lay awake all night wondering if McCree believed them, and if he did, then I began to wonder about the intensity of my original reaction to him. Why had Mama been at that concert, sitting behind us where she could watch us all evening? If she could control chance with her magic—at last I let the scary question surface: *What if she had caused the whole evening's sequence of improbable events?*

And I did mean without paying anyone off under the table!

My mental model of the universe—acquired over eight long years in four colleges—had no room in it for the will of one person to affect the life of another. Such a power couldn't exist, therefore my mother didn't have it, therefore she was a charlatan or a fool.

I tried to force myself to face it but I only ended up crying wretchedly until sunrise. The anguished knot in my gut screamed out for some concrete proof, one way or the other. I didn't know how much longer I could live with this. *"I don't care what it costs,"* I finally said aloud, *"I've got to know."*

I pasted myself together with stiff jolts of coffee and liberal applications of makeup—and made it to work on time. As I took over the hot seat, I even felt bright enough to trust myself with the job.

Later, I was sitting in a dim corner of the canteen during my coffee break when McCree showed up with a large tablet. He turned it on and set it in front of me showing a statistical tabulation.

"Last Tuesday, when you couldn't get tickets, the odds against the Ravens inviting you to a private party were nine thousand five hundred fifty three to one—assuming you did something else to attract their attention."

I scanned the tabulation and his notes, seeing he had made the assumptions I would have made. I wanted to kiss him. No, I wanted him to kiss me. But I told my heart to shut up, and I listened.

"The odds were still over a thousand to one after the concert," he said. "I guesstimated the number of cars on the street and looked up the number of cabs working, then figured the mean-free-path of the two cars, and all the routes we could have chosen. It *could* have happened once, Mavrana, but if you make a habit of this sort of thing, the odds go up steeply...."

His tentative ending was a probe. I don't know why I said it—I never seemed to be myself around McCree—but I blurted, "Yeah, it's the story of my life. My mother claims she's a witch, and she makes all these things happen to me!"

"Mavrana, be serious!"

"I am." He believed me, and his gaze changed subtly. Somehow, I had gone from fascinating woman to interesting experiment. "Look," I said, "I'm due back in the hot seat. I want to take this home and really read it.

Send it to me, OK?"

"Take the tablet. It's mine, not company property. Give it back when you're done."

As I passed my office, I dumped his tablet on my desk, wondering why I was fleeing McCree. He wasn't credulous—but he wasn't scornful either. That was chilling.

It was a singularly uneventful morning in the pit. I had made arrangements for the Ravens' visit that morning, when I arrived. At my two o'clock break, I made sure they were met at the gate and given our best tour guide. I couldn't show them around myself—the insurance law required me to be within two minutes of the hot seat at all times.

The guide was explaining that point just as he brought the Ravens into the hotbed. I relinquished my seat to my number two, and went to greet them. Phil scooped me into his arms and gave me a kiss on the cheek. So did the other Ravens, as if I were a long lost cousin, not a near stranger.

In the time it took me to recover, aware of the eyes on me, Art said, "This looks just like the auxiliary control room out on the edge."

He meant the backseat, so I said, "Yes, in case of ultimate disaster—a meltdown or major contamination—we could retreat past four more safety containments to the outer control you saw on your way in. It's identical to this one in capability, except that their view of the pit is on screens. Here we have direct vision—a bit of a luxury."

They crowded around the window, and that's when it happened.

A deep rumble, as if a truck were passing—but it grew to sound like a large freight train. Then the ceiling shook. With a loud report, a jagged crack appeared across the inner glass of the window and water began to leak from between the panes—radiation, too, no doubt but I couldn't hear the counters over the roar.

Another crack on the outer pane spurted water in a shower down into the pit, but you could barely see it for the billowing clouds of steam.

The Ravens tumbled back from the window, tangling with two of my desk men. Everyone was bewildered, paralyzed by the shock. I, however, had just come from the west coast. "Earthquake!" I shouted over the din and leaped into the hot seat, yelling, "Dan, bluephone for a complete shutdown. Max, yellowphone the Mayor an evacuation alert. Jill, redphone the grid we're going offline. Ken, what have you got?"

Ken flashed me his display, the flowchart for the whole plant. It showed line ruptures, valves opening to dump working fluids into containment, and other valves shutting down—but if those readings were correct, there wouldn't be any steam in the pit. My own monitors showed radiation rising in the hotbed. "Louanne, prepare to evacuate us to the backseat."

Frantically disciplined activity broke out as automatic commands seemed to issue themselves. Emotionally, I hadn't yet assimilated the fact that an earthquake—of better than five on the Richter scale—had just torn apart a plant on a seismically stable site.

Down in the pit ponderous machinery had begun to move along overhead tracks. The Pot was being shut down, but it would take hours to douse that sun, and we were losing coolant like crazy. The emergency crews were down there working, men and women paid, to stand by on the off chance they'd have to risk—or give—their lives to contain an accident.

I picked up the orange phone as my colleagues began to herd the Ravens out our emergency exit to the backseat despite the trembling floor. "This is an all-out Alert." I shoved my ID tag onto the plate and the phone glowed. Machinery was set in motion to bring every possible expert into our problem, either in person or on a conference line.

Then I called the President. Of the United States, that is. And it was no drill. I'd never actually done that before. I got him on his cell phone.

I was the last one out of there. The floor had stopped shaking.

My radiation tag had taken on a sickly color, but I had no time to worry about it.

In the backseat, the readouts made more sense. Somehow, the main server had been damaged but the backup was working. *God help us.*

As we completed our first emergency drills, the executive conference was convened in the deep bunker. I'd sent the Ravens to the infirmary because the Plant was now under strict quarantine. *Nothing* would leave until this was over.

I was the first to report. Standing up with all those hard eyes on me, I was more nervous than I'd been during my first solo in the hotseat. After me, damage control, Pot management, and power disbursement reported—and none of them was critical of my actions.

Doctor Howard Conwell, *the* ultimate authority in charge of the entire operation, said quietly, "Well done, all of you. So far, no stray radiation has been detected offsite. Our job is to see that none ever is. Clear?"

We all nodded. I didn't envy Conwell his job. *He* would have to stand accountable, for everything *we* had done and explain it all to the President. For the first time, I realized that *his* was the job I had been ultimately aiming for. I wasn't too sure I wanted it anymore.

In the backseat, a tense hush had fallen. We had all changed into fresh hotsuits, and been treated by the duty physicians. I had reached my exposure limit, but was still just barely safe.

What it came down to, three grueling hours later, was one tertiary backup valve. The two others that were supposed to do the job had been ruined by the quake. And the third one had not functioned. We didn't know why. Conwell had not yet ordered a suicide mission in there to ascertain why.

A quiet voice said at my elbow, "There's somebody here who insists on seeing you."

It was McCree. Behind him, flanked by Phil and Art Raven, stood my mother. She beamed pleasantly, "And look who I found!" she said gesturing to the Ravens.

"Just when I needed them."

As I stared at the three of them, it all came into focus. The earthquake had produced the exact damage we had drilled to handle in my earthquake scenario. And I remembered mother saying, *"What do I have to do, trigger an earthquake under Sterling Bridge before you'll admit the obvious?"*

McCree said "She was just applying for admittance at the main gate when the quake hit. Your 'all-out' sealed her in. I haven't had time to run a probability calculation on that one."

Mama said, "Mr. McCree has been nice enough to explain your problem to me. I want to help."

A bubble of hysterical laughter formed under my diaphragm.

McCree added, "If it might head off a dirty accident, it ought to be tried."

"Dirty" was absolutely the most powerful expletive in our jargon. "Do you have any idea what kind of help she's offering?" I asked tightly.

"I've explained the nature of my craft to him," answered Mama. She was in one of her distant-calm moods, as if not quite connected into reality. It wasn't drug induced; she never used mooders.

"I think we ought to discuss this in the conference room."

McCree objected. "There's no time! Proceed on my personal authority."

"I can't! Redlaw is in effect now, and *I'm* in the hotseat. I can't—and won't pass the buck."

"Look—what harm can it do?" asked McCree. "All she wants is a couple of square feet of space and a moment or two of silence."

I met Mama's eyes. McCree had the right attitude—scientific curiosity, not—fear. *God, I admire that man!* "All right," I said with a shrug. "But if the valve suddenly starts to work, it won't have proved anything."

"No," he agreed readily, "but it *would* be another wild improbability to add to the list. Besides, I'd like to see what's going to happen—wouldn't you?"

No. The feeling washed over me as I said, "Why not?" Somehow, I knew what was going to happen. And if it did, then maybe I'd have to abandon my whole model of the universe.

I issued orders to clear a space in the middle of the floor. "Go ahead and do your thing," I said to my mother, "but don't be surprised if we have to interrupt you with reports. Our work can't be delayed."

"I do understand," she said. "Just show me which of these screens depicts the valve in question."

McCree pointed to the main monitor that replaced the window. "It's here," he said, touching the spot where colored lines crisscrossed. The valve marked ought to have dumped the hot coolant into containment and let cold fluid into the system. "If it doesn't respond within the next hour, Conwell is going to order the suicide crew in to fix it."

I glanced at the creeping temperature readouts. We might have an hour left at that—then again, we might not.

"And where is the control for that motor-valve system?" asked Mama.

My hand went to it automatically. McCree said, "Dan Ackers there has one, and Mavrana has the master control."

"Good. When I give the word, I want both of you to work your controls to signal the valve open. And the valve will open."

She was dressed in a dark blue business suit with a light yellow blouse. As she spoke, she took the jacket off, rolled up her sleeves and stepped out of her plain navy pumps. From her leather handbag, she took a silver ring and put it on her right index finger. Laying aside her glasses, she turned to the Ravens. "Now, as I explained before, give me an A-note."

Phil hummed the note, and Art joined, and the two of them took turns breathing to sustain the note.

Mother paced out her working space, then stood to face each of the cardinal compass points in turn, gesturing. Her face had smoothed to look ten years younger, and her eyes were half closed. In that state, she began to turn in place, her arms crooked outward at shoulder height. I knew it must hurt her arthritis.

As she turned, her body seemed to blur, as if she were surrounded by a transparent cape. I blinked the illusion aside, and scanned the instruments tripping the valve switch again. But none of the indicators changed.

Everyone was staring fixedly at mother, abstract expressions on their faces. The Ravens had their heads together, eyes closed in concentration, oblivious to their surroundings. Mother spun like a corkscrew, also oblivious. Two minutes and thirty-five seconds had passed when mother began to Sing. It was a word that sounded like all vowels, enunciated not with the mouth but with the gut. I felt my bones vibrating, and my brain tingling.

Then she was still, the ringed finger pointing at me. "Signal and the valve will function."

I wanted to laugh it away, but McCree was staring at me intently. I tripped the valve control again, and mother jerked around to point at Dan. "Signal—now!"

His eyes had dilated and he seemed to be staring at the end of her finger. But his hand moved to the control.

I was afraid to look at the main screen.

Mother moved to the Ravens, put one hand on a shoulder of each of them and brought them out of their trance, cutting off the A tone so suddenly everything changed.

McCree whispered reverently, "Dear God!"

On the main screen, the readout had shifted colors and symbols to show the valve was open. Coolant was moving.

I didn't believe it. It was just the computer readout. I flipped the displays until we were watching the pit. The plume of steam from the safety bleeder was waning. As we watched, it stopped. That had to mean the pressure was down and the coolant was being dumped—at last—into the pressure container designed to hold it.

In the awed silence, Jill said, "The temperature at

the periphery has stopped rising."

At intervals during the next half hour, she reported as the other temperature monitors leveled off. It would be days until the actual pile temperature would go down, but we knew we'd won when the last of her monitors leveled.

The cheer was deafening.

At the executive conference that night, Conwell said, "You're all to be commended to the United Nations for preventing even a single death or injury during the worst fusion disaster in history." What he meant was that, because of our efficiency, his neck wasn't on the chopping block.

As soon as I could, I confronted Mama. "I'm still, not convinced—so what are you going to do next time, bring a meteor down on top of us?"

She looked shocked. "Mavrana, you can't think that we *caused* the earthquake?"

"I recall that you *said* you would."

"That was just to plant the idea in your mind to drill them for it. Our astrologer and three of our best psychics predicted it just after they built the plant, so our group has been working hard to prevent a real disaster."

Relieved and exasperated, I threw my hands up and walked away. Later, McCree brought in a printout of the probability estimates for this long chain of events. When I saw the actual figures in cold print, something snapped. In the scientific view of the universe, improbable events just do not happen in such long chains just for the convenience of man. There has to be some relationship between science and magic—and I'm going to find it.

The search will be quite a lot of fun since McCree has agreed to work with me, even after hours.

EVENT AT HOLIDAY ROCK

Most people say it was a coincidence, but I know differently, and I think it's time I told the whole story.

It was just three years ago today that it happened. At the time, I, Charlie Collins, was Chief Musician at the Rock, and I was scheduled to play the last Sunset Concert before they closed the new dam and inundated all of Boiling Rock Basin and most of Holiday Rock with it.

That would be an awesome sight. It never rained in Boiling Rock Basin, but the Basin was really a huge tilted plane, walled by mountains that funneled the northern runoff into the South Sea on Hobart's Hearth. Offworld tourists would sit in hoverbubbles to watch the first rain of winter when the Rock was closed, and a hundred-meter-high wall of water would come crashing down that tilted funnel. The engineers who built the dam across Sluice Gap Narrows swore the thing would stop any wall of water the north country could throw down—but I had my doubts.

The day of my last concert, the fire-blue sky was as starkly bare of clouds as ever. I stood at the foot of the Rock, blinking away tears of nostalgia and trying to imagine how high on the two-hundred-meter columns of the Rock the water would come. Looking up at the spires, resplendent in heat shimmer and their natural rainbow colors, I tried to imagine what the long-dead alien builders would have thought of us for drowning their one surviving artifact.

I was in no hurry to go into the control room. The tourist buses were bringing my last audience, the most distinguished group I've ever played to: two hundred Heads of State, Personages, Personalities, and Influentials.

They straggled across the blue, red, and black drystone toward the arena, making tourist noises at the awesome columns and sweating in the dry desert heat, envying their native guides' dry foreheads. With them came troops of reporters, followed by teams wrestling with the best professional recording gear available anywhere in the galaxy—none of the usual pocketcorders the amateurs dragged along, but real professional equipment in professional hands. And this last time, I wanted to be in absolute top form.

I'd always wanted to be a legitimate musician, but I didn't have the money to go to study at offworld conservatories. I was twenty-two then, and I calculated I'd be sixty-three before I'd have the money. So I was determined to be noticed at this last Sunset Concert.

The cliff shadows were creeping toward the arena where the dignitaries and reporters were jostling for seats. I licked dry lips and crossed the expanse of crushed black stone to the base of the Rock. The tremendous pillars of stone that buttressed the Rock rose directly, in sheer massiveness, out of the flat gravel base. It was like walking between the feet of some god-sized statue hewn from wind-carved stone.

As I moved into the dim tunnels, the grim tension drained out of me, replaced as always by quiet awe. I had to pause one last time at the Inscription Room. I had spent more time there than any offworld scholar doing a paper on the Rock.

Each of the four Inscriptions is a short message followed by a long, intricate musical score. "Those who sit, silently, attentive to every note of the Sunset Concert will experience good luck for a time proportionate to the degree of their concentration. Those who think of other things will experience bad luck and failure for a similarly proportionate time."

We only play the Rock at sunset, but the aliens had other appointed times. "Those who dance to the Dawn Concert will have long lives and good health in proportion to their skill. Those who sit at the Dawn Concert will die young."

The Midnight Concert was for those who would know God and the Noon Concert for those who would marry and establish a dynasty. Standing among the ornately carved pillars of the Inscription Room, vibrating with echoes of the Rock's sepulchral tones, it was easy to believe that hearing this instrument could be a blessing or a curse, as you willed it.

My theory was that the Inscriptions applied only when the music inscribed on those mysteriously durable plaques was played at the correct time of day.

I'd learned to play what I thought was a good imitation of the Dawn Concert...it surely sounded weird enough to be alien music...and I'd played it occasionally as part of the Sunset Concert along with the usual Bach adaptations and folk medleys. The year before, I'd mastered the Noon Concert, and this last year before the scheduled inundation, I'd been working on the Sunset Concert. I thought I had it down pretty close to what the aliens intended, but I'd never had the courage to play it at sunset. Until now. I was out of a job—and I needed luck.

I pulled myself away from the Inscription Room and entered the Control Room through the concealed door behind the fake end of the corridor. As I took my place at the enormous keyboard, shaking in fear of what I was about to do, I kept thinking that if my theory was correct and the Eminent Leaders of this entire Stellar Sector didn't listen to the concert attentively, I could be responsible for—God alone knew what.

The easy familiarity of the hand-sized keys, the huge foot pedals, and the maze of knobs that controlled the giant wind organ finally exerted their calming influence as I faced the imminence of a performance. The reporters outside were already broadcasting or recording their lead-up to the announcement that this would be the first and the last public performance of the Sunset Concert by human hands, a final and fitting tribute to Holiday Rock.

I watched the Sunset Hole above me. When the

shadow line darkened, I would have to sound the first chord or the timing would be off and the music ineffective. And as I watched, I prayed.

I don't know to whom or what I prayed, but it was the most fervent prayer of my life—that the dignitaries out there would take this seriously—that somehow, someday, I would play my beloved Rock again—that through some miracle I'd be able to attend a proper conservatory and really learn music.

And then the bright spot of light winked out, and almost without my volition, my hands and feet coordinated in creating that first, spine-chilling, hair-raising chord. I remember being aware, as I heard and felt the awesome tones take shape from the winds, of a wondrous light feeling, as if a staggering burden had been lifted off me.

I played the Sunset Concert as I'd never played it—or anything else—before, with a totally enraptured concentration, listening to the music I created rather than concentrating on the mechanics of creating it. I never once looked at my score. I was completely caught up in the soaring, single-key melodies building one after another, a structure of interwoven towers behind ethereal veils; building and combining, splitting and rejoining into ever greater crescendos, and finally culminating in one glorious all-consuming symbolic wholeness, a complex chord involving almost the entire tonal range of the Rock.

The reverberations died away, leaving a terrible silence that could only be described as pregnant. I don't know how long I sat there, mind and senses benumbed, unable to move or think, almost totally unaware of my surroundings, before it happened.

At first, I thought it was residual vibrations from the music, but in a few seconds, the creaking, shaking, and swaying reached terrifying proportions. I clutched my bench, eyeing the ceiling distrustfully, heedless of the powdered rock sifting into my eyes. Quakes were no strangers to me. Where I grew up, they were practically a daily occurrence. But here in Boiling Rock Basin, they simply never happened. The region was certified seismically stable.

It lasted about four minutes, and I judged it at about eight on the ten-scale. I wasn't far wrong; it turned out to be eight point seven. Which was enough to thoroughly ruin that multi-billion credit dam.

Now, you go ahead and tell me it was a coincidence. But if you do, I'll bet my Conservatory Scholarship and my Debut Contract you haven't been tallying the stories the Newsnets, have been carrying about the highly improbable good fortunes of the Eminent Leaders of this Stellar Sector.

Would you have the courage to rebuild that dam?

AVENTURA

I was enchanting the raisin bread when the boss called me to the phone. I worked in a commercial bakery then. I'd been promoted to raisin bread and jelly donuts because I could preserve the raisins' plumpness and the dough's yeasty freshness for two weeks on the store shelves. I could do a hundred forty-four jelly donuts at once, and keep the jelly hot and the icing just right for eight days.

The job paid poorly, and there was no future in it. At twenty-four, I was already a top bakery enchanter. But I expected to quit at the end of the month to get married. So when the boss called me to the phone, I thought it was the wedding caterer.

"Miss Tira Nau?" asked a voice.

"Yes."

"This is Forbes, of Forbes, Gibbon and Reilly, attorneys for the Prosper Nau Estate. We'd like you to come to our office on a matter concerning your uncle's will."

My father's older brother, Prosper had died a year ago. He'd split with my father long before my father, who scorned magical education, was killed when a fireworks plant lost control of a fire elemental. A cousin had told me Prosper, a Certified Public Wizard, had died never knowing his brother was dead because he'd warded himself against hearing his brother's name.

"Where are you located?" I asked.

He told me. It would take an hour to get there on the public bus. "I can make it at five tomorrow."

"Fine. I'll wait for you." He gave me directions.

I scribbled them down, and said I'd be there.

The attorney's offices were typical of any wizard class business—sedate, staid navy blue and silver carpets and drapes, with snow-cloud grey plush furniture. The blond receptionist showed me into a huge office where Forbes sat behind a desk bigger than my apartment's living room.

The desk was hand-chipped obsidian, of course, and utterly bare except for a gleaming white Paraphernalia Case about five feet by two feet. Behind the case sat the wizard, wearing his peaked cap and long black robe, as if he were in court.

"Please be seated, Miss Nau. These proceedings are being recorded for the court records."

I swallowed my nerves, perched on the edge of the visitor's chair, and pretended he didn't intimidate me. How could they hold me liable for Uncle Prosper's debts?

He told me my uncle's will dispersed his considerable wealth to various charities for underprivileged magicians, but specified that this one item should go to his wayward but talented brother, who refused to practice the craft.

Then he shoved the white case toward me. "Since you are your father's only heir, this now belongs to you."

Not without trepidation, I opened it.

Inside was a sword shaped from translucent quartz flecked with gold. The guard and pommel were jeweled, and carved, and the whole thing glowed with power. It was a magical Implement such as only the most accomplished could use, and only the most affluent could afford.

Hesitantly, I picked it up. The charge tingled along my arms and made my hair stand on end. I could enchant the entire bakery's produce for the day with this! "Oh, I don't—this couldn't—I couldn't there must be some mistake!"

"No, indeed. Hold the sword vertically."

I did, feeling it resist being turned; then it leaped from my hands to hover before me. A small area cleared in the blade, and suddenly I was looking at my uncle's face.

"Greetings, Gil. As you receive this small bequest, please believe that I wish you only happiness. This sword is called Aventura. Perhaps it will bring you freedom. Blessings be...." The eyes squinted, as if trying to make out something blurry. "...on you and your progeny."

The picture flickered out. I suppressed a shiver as I said to the wizard, "I can't—"

"Well, you needn't use it. You can store it and bequeath it to your children." He closed the Case. "You did say you were busy, so I won't detain—"

"Doesn't the Case come with it?"

"Oh, no—that belongs to the firm. But Paraphernalia Cases can be purchased—"

"I know," I replied, standing up, for twice my annual salary! The sword bobbed to my shoulder height, still glowing with that luminous charge. Perhaps I could use it in my hall as a coat tree? "Is there an owner's manual?"

"No, this is all we received. It's quite old. The original papers have long since disintegrated. You can look it up in any good reference. Or—as any quality item of the sort, it will be glad to instruct you."

"I see." I didn't. "Well, thank you, Mr. Forbes."

Out on the street, I felt self-conscious with the quartz sword following at my shoulder. People who owned such things had their own limousines. I had to take a crowded bus.

I tried to ignore the stares Aventura collected as I dropped coins into the slot. People standing in the aisle stared and made way to let me through. A seat was vacated near the back door, and I swooped into it, trapping the sword next to the window.

It was a long ride across town. We passed through the university section. The bus emptied, and students piled on. The sword attracted only mild curiosity here.

Finally, one woman student asked, "May I sit here, Professor?"

Professor? "Oh, uh, certainly." Who else but a professor could look so seedy and own such an

Implement?

Politely, the student asked, "It's an Attitudinal, isn't it? Finnish manufacture?"

"Um." I was embarrassed at how little I knew.

"Will you be teaching with it next semester?" At my confusion, she apologized. "I'm interested in Attitudinals. I'm majoring in Social Work."

"I see," I replied. My own education included only two years of Enchanter's Trade School.

"I'm in organic chemistry, actually. Reaction Arrestment specialist."

As we talked, new notions awakened in the back of my mind. By the time she got off, I could see myself married, raising kids, and working for a Wizardship. I wondered where I'd get the money. Aventura wasn't the sort of thing one could sell. Um, I'd have to master it before I could pass it on to another owner who wasn't my child.

My fiancé, Rogero, was waiting when I arrived at the jewelry store where we were to pick up our wedding rings. We'd chosen them on an auspicious day a month ago, and they'd been sent out to the Monogramming Sorcerer. Rogero had ordered mine set to record permanently how I looked the moment he put the ring on my finger; and he'd paid extra to have an anti-loss spell put on it.

He looked dapper in his neat, black suit and ever-clean patent shoes. He carried a businessman's Paraphernalia Case made of dark purple leather, with a woven shoulder strap. And he was wearing the hat I'd bought him for his birthday. I felt twice as dowdy as I walked up to him, still in my bakery whites, with my old cloth coat thrown over.

He turned. "I thought you'd never—what's *that*?"

He eyed the sword bobbing at my shoulder. I told him, adding, "An hour ago, I'd no idea what to do with it. Now, I'm thinking I'll go back to school and learn to use it."

He shook his head, saying, "Well, come on, let's get the rings before the store closes."

It was early autumn, and already getting dark. We inspected the rings, and signed for them, as the jeweler admired Aventura, and tried to sell us a more expensive wedding band set. Hiding exasperation, Rogero put him off.

Out on the street, he fumed, "You've got to get rid of that thing."

That had been my goal since I first saw it. But when Rogero made it an edict I rebelled. "Why? It could be useful. It got me a seat on the bus!"

"Tira, it's going to be nothing but trouble." He walked around it, inspecting it, as passers-by gave it a wide berth. "How do you turn it off?"

"I don't know. It didn't come with a manual. I'll have to do some research."

"Where will you get the time! I'm not having tha— that thing—bobbing along our honeymoon!"

"Now wait a minute!" His attitude made me angry. Aventura bobbed faster and began to glow more brightly.

Rogero sighed, gesturing placatingly. "It's all right, Tira. I've got connections. I'll find out how to turn it off for you. Then we can pack it away and forget it. Come on." He turned toward the subway.

"Where are we—?" I started, hanging back. Aventura made a menacing twang at Rogero.

He stopped in the middle of the sidewalk, exasperated. "I had this evening all planned to be one of the happiest memories of our lives. Tira, we've got celebrating to do—I've been promoted!"

"Then you got the Infant's Clothing Department?" It was a plum of a job for a fireproofing charmer because of the cost of manufacturer's liability insurance; it was a responsible, well paid, management position.

He took my shoulders, glaring at Aventura. "No! I'm now Managing Charmer of the Commercial Textile department. The Chief Sorcerer took me aside and told me I could've had the post anytime these last two years, but they wanted a stable, married man. So it's all your doing, and I'm going to take you out on the town!"

I squealed my delight, and kissed him. "What a piece of luck. Now we can afford university courses!"

"Anything you want, Tira—anything." He pulled me toward the subway. But as we flowed down the stairs with the rest of the crowd, he muttered, "I just don't think you're going to have time, though."

Since I'd be quitting my job, I didn't see what I'd have except time, but I didn't argue; no point spoiling his mood.

He took me home, and I dressed in my best. As we left my apartment, the sword insisted on following. I tried standing on the threshold and slamming the door before the sword could squeeze through after me, but it danced and slithered through. Once I caught it between the door and the jamb, but it resisted being crushed and popped out after me, flickering brightly, as if proud of itself.

Rogero and I tried all the spells we could think of to turn it off, which was a lot, since he had two years more school than I. "It's no good," he admitted at last. "We'll miss the show if we don't get going. Just ignore it."

"Can you?" Aventura seemed to intimidate him.

"Certainly," he said, and kissed me.

I thereupon forgot everything, and followed happily.

As always, he was as good as his word. Aventura hovered behind my aisle seat at the play (to which Rogero had been given tickets); stationed itself behind my chair at the restaurant, and bobbed rhythmically when we danced.

He acknowledged it only when people from his firm came up to congratulate him, and inquired about it. "My fiancé inherited it," he'd say, and steer the conversation away.

At midnight, I yawned, and said, "It's getting late, and I have to be at work early in the morning."

"I hadn't thought! I'm sorry, Tira." He called for the check.

As we collected our coats, one of his bosses came in,

congratulated him, and was introduced to me. As we were leaving, Rogero said, "This is why you've got to quit that job. I can't afford to leave now. To get beyond lower management without a Sorcerer's Certificate, I've got to make all the right contacts. I don't have to be at work until noon."

In the cab, I fell into a strange mood. I'd always had such deliriously happy times with Rogero—parties at rich friends' houses, restaurants and theaters—places I couldn't afford. We always met exciting, important people who made me feel wonderful. Tonight had been even better because Rogero was a center of attention. But I didn't feel good about it.

I was annoyed, peeved, and rebellious. I suddenly couldn't see spending the rest of my life as Rogero's smiling and witty decoration. I'd be no more to him, after a few years, than Aventura—an accoutrement that should be turned off when convenient. Suddenly, *I* wanted to be important.

I kissed him goodnight, but my heart wasn't in it.

I lay awake, my nice dark bedroom glowing with the sword's light. The darn thing even followed me into the bathroom!

In the morning, I couldn't get the sword to stay home. I tried explaining to it, calling it by name, and even asking it for instructions on how to get it to stay home. But it still dogged my steps. I tried slamming the door on it again, and almost broke my wrist. Finally, I ran for my bus and just made it to work on time.

I was so tired from the late night, I didn't even

notice the swirling mutter of comments following me across the floor to my station. I climbed up to survey the conveyor belt. The first rank of raisin breads was still ten minutes away.

Wishing I'd had time for another cup of coffee, I tooled up and got ready to cast my freshness enchantment, wondering how I'd muddle through the day. I didn't want to get fired before I quit—I might need the recommendation some day. So I pulled myself together and began to raise my cone of power. I was so fuzzy-minded, this would take all my energy.

The ranks of loaves arrived, and I enchanted. I picked up the familiar rhythm and began to feel jaunty. I could do this in my sleep. Surely I could get a Charmer Degree.

I prepared to shift to jelly donuts, when coffee break time came and the boss called me to his office. He had a tray of unrisen, unbaked raisin loaves on his desk.

Eyeing Aventura, he asked, "Would you mind explaining just what is going on around here?"

I started to tell him about the lawyer, and how Rogero and I had tried to turn the sword off.

"I didn't mean the sword, Miss Nau. I meant this!"

"That's raisin bread."

"No, that's dough."

"Well—give it time," I suggested lamely.

"Miss Nau, this bread rose and was baked this morning. It passed your station at nine-fifteen and entered the wrapping plant in this condition! You did this, Miss Nau. Eighteen hundred loaves that cannot be baked—according to our lab analysis—for another two weeks, because of your ultra-freshness spell!"

He'd become more livid as he spoke, and I felt the old shiver of intimidation start. Something snapped inside me. "Well then," I quipped, "sell it as bake-at-home!"

"I don't have to take lip from a 'chanter! You're fired, Miss Nau, effective this minute! Pick up your pay and leave—and take that with you!" He gestured to the sword.

Aventura spat sparks at him, very much as I wished I could. I turned and stalked out of the office, and across the floor, without speaking to any of my friends. I picked up my pay, and, as I cleaned out my locker, Myra, who 'chanted the hot buttered toast, came over.

"What happened, Tira?" She eyed the sword.

"Got fired." I refused to cry. Myra wanted to console me, invite me over to dinner. I explained about the sword, and said, "I've got a million things to do. I'll call you."

I walked to the bus stop, berating myself. I knew better than to snap at a manager during a richly deserved reprimand. But maybe one 'chanter in a hundred could have done what I did—even if it wasn't the job I was hired for. Maybe I'd snapped at the boss because I'd been feeling important, like the people Rogero knew. But I wasn't really that good, only a little better than I'd been yesterday. Yet—no, I'd have known if the sword had amplified my enchantment. I'd done it all myself.

Still, I'd never have done it without the sword. Rogero was right: I had to turn it off before it made chaos of my life.

I got off the bus at the university and bought a campus library card.

After an hour of fruitless labor, I asked for help. It took three librarians another hour to locate the history of Aventura. With copies of those pages and a stack of books, I found a nook among some lawn statuary where I could sit in the afternoon sun, sheltered from the wind, and read.

Aventura was easily a thousand years old, but the books only traced it back to the Magical Renaissance. I'd been right, one had to master it to pass it on.

As an "Attitudinal," it operated on the psyche, not the physical world. It didn't add power to the magician's work, but helped the magician tap his own. Uncle Prosper's words suddenly made sense: he'd willed Aventura to my father to induce my father to change his attitude about magic. Now, it seemed to be changing mine. And the only way I could make it stop was by mastering it.

I'd never done well in school. I'd almost flunked out of Enchanter's Trade School. But perhaps I hadn't done well because I didn't think enough of myself. I mused on this until shadows crept over my toes; then I strode over to the administration building and picked up some catalogs.

I caught an express bus home in time to meet Rogero. He was going to help me sort my junk and pack what I needed off to his apartment, which was much larger than mine.

When I arrived, he was pacing back and forth in front of my door. Dressed in his immaculate blue suit and white shirt, with navy shoes and hat; he carried a large bundle (probably work clothes), and his Paraphernalia Case was bulging.

I came toward him brimming over with good news, and started to babble out all I'd discovered.

He cut me off. "Where've you been? I've been waiting for half an hour!" I could hear how offended he was.

My head was full of muzzy plans for unlocking my latent talents. I'd even daydreamed of becoming a professor. But I leashed back my temper, offering my armload of reference books. "At the university. Research."

"You took off from work?"

I confessed I'd been fired for cause.

"Fired? Insubordination?"

"Rogero, he had a right to fire me. There are thousands who could replace me." Tears sprang to my eyes. I'd never been fired before, and I felt humiliated.

I sniffed, holding my breath against the urge to sob. Rogero put an arm around me, his whole attitude melting into protectiveness. Strangely, I felt it was as if he'd always expected me to fail, and it was his prerogative to comfort me when that happened—like a retarded child. Just as my father always had comforted me. *Is this why I've never felt my own power? I've soaked up my father's attitude toward me, fulfilling his unconscious expectations?*

"There, now, feel better?" he asked, taking the key from my hand and opening the door. As we went on in, dumping our things in the living room, he said, "While you start dinner, I'll see what we can do about this sword. We'll have it whipped in an hour or so."

I went cold all over. He wasn't even looking to see what I'd brought home. He would rely on his friends, and his contacts, and his knowledge, as if mine didn't exist.

True, I didn't move in the kind of exalted circles he did. He could probably find out from a wizard friend what I'd be charged a bundle for in an office consultation—and he could use what he found out. But—I paused in the kitchen door. "Rogero, you know Aventura is my sword, and I don't think anyone else is going to be able to affect it."

"I'll call you when I need you."

He's going to call me when he needs me. Now doesn't that summarize our entire relationship! He did things, and called me when he needed me. When he didn't need me, I should be put away in a closet. I don't know why I hadn't seen it before. It was as plain as my nose reflected in Aventura's blade.

He started to spread a symbol cloth on the floor, consulting a diagram drawn on a napkin.

"That seems awfully elaborate, just to find the off-spell for an Implement," I observed.

"How many swords like this have you seen turned off?"

"Probably as many as you have!"

Exasperated, he said, "Look, I know what I'm doing. Leonardo explained it to me, step by step."

"So explain it to me."

"You wouldn't understand."

"Try me."

"Tira, we don't have all night."

"I just wanted to make sure it wouldn't get damaged."

"Now, how could you think I'd do anything like that? That's a valuable antique, and it will add a certain— elegance—displayed in our living room."

"Our living room," I repeated. Always before, those words had lit in me a warm wriggling of anticipation and happiness; but, suddenly, I heard what he himself didn't know he was saying. It was his living room, and I was his, and my sword was his, and we'd both be displayed there. "My Implement will add a touch of elegance to your living room."

He put one hand on a hip, and cocked his head aside. "What has gotten into you? All last night, and now this. That sword is ruining your attitude."

"Ruining my.... Suppose I like my new attitude?"

He said, softly, as if speaking to an excitable mental patient, "That could be the sword talking, not you. Now, just be calm a while, and we'll have it turned off and put away. And then you'll be your old self."

"Suppose I don't want to be my old self? Suppose I want to turn Aventura back on again?"

"Tira, neither of us has the training to wield it. It's already got us fighting. It's best to be laid aside."

"Who are you to decide what's 'best,' and without

even consulting me!"

"Your fiancé, that's who. In just a few days, we'll be married. With this new promotion, I'll be able to move you into a lovely house. And with you by my side, there's no limit to where I can go in the company. They're already talking about sending me to the West Coast."

My whole vision of married life crashed around my ears. "I can't go to the coast if I'm in the middle of college here!" My voice was loud enough now for the neighbors to hear, but I didn't care.

"It doesn't matter. There are schools out west." He kept his voice down, but the effort made him growl.

It was clear he didn't think any more of my chances in school than my father had. No, I didn't have the strength to fight that every day and night. "Maybe we better get this straight right now. I decide what's to be done with and to Aventura. I decide what school I'm going to, what I'm going to major in, when I'm going to move, and where I'm moving to. If it's not convenient, you can adjust to it. Maybe you'll have to go on to the coast for a year or two without me."

"Tira, you're out of your mind! There's no point my going anywhere without you! Who would entertain for me? How would I get ahead? What would people think?"

"That I have a career of my own?" There was an edge to my voice. "And who's going to entertain for me? How am I going to get ahead?"

He frowned, as if suddenly hearing me for the first

time. "Are you telling me you don't want to marry me?"

I heard myself for the first time. Choking back disgraceful tears, I said, "No, but I don't want to marry anyone who doesn't know I exist."

"What an awful thing to say!" Now he was yelling, deeply offended. "I've spent hours today taking care of your problems. You're practically all I've thought about for months and months now. Everything I do is for you!"

"Which makes me some kind of burden!" *That's how Dad always thought of me—a chore, a burden.*

"Is that why you want to go back to school? So you don't need me to do things for you?"

I snapped, without thinking, "That'd scare you, wouldn't it? Well, I've decided I'm going to get my Wizardry Degree, and if you don't like it, there's the door!"

He stood dumbfounded for a moment. "You think it'll be that easy?" He gathered up his cloth, saying, "Well, it's not, Tira. You're making a big mistake. You'll never even pass the entry exams. And now you've been fired," he added ramming his hat on his head, "you'll never get another decent 'chanter's job. You'll live the rest of your life on public assistance. Mark my words. Goodbye!"

The door slammed with total finality and I crumpled into a heap, and sobbed my heart out. It was only afterwards that I realized Aventura hadn't spat sparks at him. It just hung in the air, barely glowing—letting me fight my own battle.

Since I'd given notice as of my wedding date, the landlord had already rented my apartment to an elderly gentleman. I couldn't get it back. So I went apartment and job shopping near campus. Bus fare ate into my small savings, and what I could get from selling the ring I'd bought for Rogero. I wondered how I was going to survive.

Nights I lay awake, hungry because I was chintzing on meals—besides, I could afford to lose a few pounds—and alternately wishing Rogero would call and make up, and exulting in my fortitude in not calling him. I wanted to be established before he called, or I knew I'd fall weakly into his arms and let him turn Aventura off. And I'd hate myself for the rest of my life.

I began to talk to that sword, telling it my troubles as if it could understand why I couldn't face any of my friends from the bakery until I was settled. Rogero's parents had a secretary who'd do the work of calling the wedding off. None of the guests were mine, anyway.

I made myself read the university library books, even when I didn't understand a word in five. I answered every ad for a part-time job in my field, and even some outside it. I filed with every agency, and went to dozens of interviews, glibly reciting the explanation that I needed the job to pay for my Wizard's Degree, dull quartz sword bobbing happily beside me. Twice I was promised a job, and then turned down—after they'd had time to check my references. I began to wonder if I should cheat and not mention the bakery, because they'd blackballed me.

The day before I was to be evicted, I went to campus to return the books. Afterwards, I crawled into the nook of the lawn sculpture where I'd first gotten the idea I could go back to school. Less than three weeks ago, I'd had a good home waiting, a solid husband, and a bright, open future. Now I was all but a vagrant without a place to sleep for the night.

But the sunset was gorgeous. The cricket song was balm to the nerves. The grass was soft and sensuous beneath my bare feet. The rough, hard granite sculpture was warm from the sun, and eased my aching back better than a heating pad. The buildings around me seemed the very definition of beauty, as they blended with the natural setting. Students strolled or bicycled or jogged about; anxious, listless, worried, or joyful, each was uniquely alive.

The world hadn't changed; I had. Suddenly, my heart was bursting with tearful gratitude that I was finally allowed to know this hidden beauty. I sat spellbound for nearly an hour, until the exquisite pain of that knowledge abated. I knew I was happy. I'd never been happy before. Better that all trace of that former life be gone.

At last, it began to get chilly. I thought of beds, breakfast, toilets. Soon the campus would be closed, the students off to their apartments or dorms.

I pulled myself to my feet, and noticed Aventura's dull light in the growing shadow. It had never so much as sparkled since the night I threw Rogero out. It seemed to have turned its back on me. I stood up, almost nose to pommel with it, and said, "Uncle Prosper, you sent me freedom and happiness—but being jobless and homeless is no blessing!" I hardly recognized my own voice. It was an octave too low, and sounded like a wizard's. "Aventura, I will not allow you to master me."

"Yes, Mistress. How may I serve?"

Stunned, trembling, for this was the first response the sword had ever made, I continued in that same tone. "Help me find a place to live, and a job."

"This way, please, Mistress."

I followed, glad Aventura didn't sound like Prosper, or my father. The sword vibrated, glowing brightly. It sounded a C natural, then tilted and picked up speed, as if homing on a beacon. I felt ridiculous, panting along behind a very conspicuous sword, calling, "Not so fast! I'm coming."

It twanged again, but went faster. It led me through tunnels of greenery, up stairs set in hillsides, across a wide glade, under some ancient trees, and to the edge of campus, where the buildings were more than a century old.

There, on the steps of a three-story brown-shingle building half smothered in old ivy, I found a young woman in flowered shorts and a scanty top, crying softly and desperately into her cupped hands. It was the woman I'd met on the bus. "Aventura," I hissed, still trying to catch my breath, "I meant paying work, not counseling distraught students."

The sword didn't answer. It had gone dull again, bobbing serenely behind me. I started to fade back into the shrubbery. Whatever her problem, I had no time or resource to help her. But that desolate sound grabbed my heart. Maybe the old me could have walked away pretending to mind my own business when I was really just intimidated by a problem bigger than I was. The new me was so sure I could help that it would be a crime to turn away.

Reluctantly, I presented myself at the bottom of the steps. She looked up, recognized the sword, and exclaimed, embarrassed, "Professor!"

"I'm no professor," I confessed. I sat down beside her, and said, "But I've done some crying in my life. Want to trade tales of woe?"

"Mine's about a man."

"Mine, too."

"Are all men like that?"

"Not any more than all women are like us."

She told me how the guy she'd been living with had pulled out, taking her things, and leaving a big rent bill, a whopping disillusionment, and a broken heart that would never mend. She ended, blowing her nose into a wad of tissues, "If I can stop crying long enough, I'm going to see if they can help." She indicated the building behind us.

I read the sign. "Campus Women's Counseling Center. What do you suppose they can do? What you need is a better paying job, not a psychologist."

"Or a new room-mate. They keep a room-mate-wanted list—what's the matter?"

"What would you think of taking in me and my

sword?"

"What?"

"I told you, I'm not a visiting professor." I sketched my story briefly. "So you see, if I can find work—"

She was eager to have me—or maybe Aventura. "They keep a jobs list inside, too—let's go!"

The place stank of dampness and disinfectant, stale coffee, and, even this late, it rang with the sounds of phones and busy people calling to each other. Hallways led in three directions, and behind an abandoned secretary's desk heaped with papers, a stairway led upwards. Bulletin boards were layers deep in old notices. The floors were tilted this way and that, as if the building had been jacked up many times, and there was a stain on the thin carpet where water had leaked through the roof.

"Come look at this—," my new friend called, then laughed. "I don't even know your name!"

"Tira Nau. Yours?"

"Nadine Shellman. Look, here's a whole kitchen outfit for sale. Norm took everything I had when he—"

"I've got tons of housekeeping stuff- I need a job."

"Which one of you said that?" came a deep voice.

I jumped, with a start, as if caught at something naughty. "I did," I admitted. Suddenly, I was intimidated, driven back to being that same, ultimate failure of a person I'd been all my life.

The woman was tall, overweight, grey haired, not very crisply groomed, but imposing in her manner. She questioned me, shotgun style. "What sort of a job?"

I listed my qualifications.

"Three years in a bakery? You a student here?"

"Not yet. I'm going to enroll next semester." I tried to hold my head high and sound as if I meant it, but my voice squeaked, and I could hear, see, and feel all the ways I'd ever projected failure to everyone I spoke to.

She quirked an eyebrow toward the sword, as if wondering what I was doing with such a powerful thing.

Slowly, it came to me that I had gotten Aventura to call me Mistress—which was more than Rogero would ever have tried for. "I've come here," I said, my voice dropping into the wizard's tone, "to master this sword. But I'm already a top freshness enchanter. I'd be valuable in the cafeteria, setting food to stay hot or cold, or preventing overcooking."

"Those jobs are usually reserved for students."

It was a cold put-off, the sort of thing that once would have made me slink away with my head between my shoulders, wondering where I'd gotten the nerve to apply in the first place. But not now.

"As they should be," I replied. "And I'm going to be a student, as soon as registration opens." I had no money, but perhaps I'd get a scholarship, or a loan. I met the woman's eyes, confident in my own powers.

She turned and shouted to someone in another room, "Forget it, Madge. The job's filled." And to me, she said, "You start tomorrow at five-thirty, preparing breakfast in the main cafeteria. I come on at six, and you'd better be there, and working. I run the place, and

I don't stand for any nonsense. Come on, I'll show you around."

I had a new boss, tougher than any I'd ever worked for; but I had a new toughness myself. *By the time she checks my references, I'll have proven myself invaluable.*

A MOTHER'S CURSE

Kimban, Guardian of the Speaker of the Village of Epo, leaned his buttocks against the table on which his silver sword rested. "Chesra, you can't wait another month. In your eighth month, an Active Speaking could kill you. You have to make your Abdication tonight, and if you get through *that* Active Speaking without fainting, I'll be amazed."

A Speaker could Speak effortlessly of that which already was, but to Speak and thus *cause* it to be so took enormous toll. Taking up or setting down the Office of Speaker meant just such an Active Speaking.

The pregnant woman's pacing shook the wooden floor. "You just want me out of the way so you can ruin Briller by declaring all the soap he's made this summer tainted."

Ignoring the slight to his oath as a Guardian, one able to See the forces of magic, Kimban replied, "Pregnancy is disrupting your stability. It isn't for you to judge now—"

Whirling on him in a fury, she spat, "You're just jealous that I carry Briller's child, not yours! That's what's behind everything you do! Well, I'm still

Speaker of Epo, and *I* say I—" She broke off, mouth open to form words, yet no voice or breath behind them. Her astonishment would have been comical had it not been so pained.

Kimban should have gone to her aid as was his duty as her Guardian, but he froze at her accusation. When she'd taken up her Office, she'd Spoken onto her own lips the Seal of Truth that had just silenced her. Therefore, her words had been true. But—*Me? Jealous? Of that worm?* And then, *Worm?* The truth seared him to the core.

Briller was nearly fifteen years older than Kimban, closer to Chesra's age. Though a Speaker never married, to Briller she owed a son, the son she now bore.

With a strangled sound, Kimban went to enfold her in his arms. The feel of her child moving against his belly almost distracted him, but he found his voice and sang the note she needed to hear. "Chesra, relax. Listen, and relax; you'll be able to breathe again. Come on, for your baby, Chesra."

She drew a tremulous breath as the door burst open, and Briller's heavy step shook the floor. The man stopped, understanding replacing anxiety. With bitter disappointment, he mumbled, "We heard raised voices. I thought the baby—"

"I'm all right," Chesra interrupted. She drew away from Kimban and stood proudly as she addressed Briller with a cold formality, "Please inform the musicians that I will conclude the Speaking tonight with my Abdication. And have the colors changed to something appropriate."

Briller executed a formal bow. "As you wish, Speaker."

Chesra added, "Briller—you are never to enter without invitation. Understand? My very life could have been at stake. If Kimban had not been so adept at his job—well, I don't want to contemplate what might have happened."

"His job," repeated Briller skeptically.

"His *job,*" she asserted. She met Briller's gaze, neither haughty nor defiant, but simply confident.

The symphony of expressions that flowed across Briller's face was indescribable. "I'll mention only his competency." Glancing at Kimban, Briller bowed to them both, and left.

Kimban felt tension he'd scarcely been aware of flow out of him. At last, his calm reasoning had won Chesra over. He hadn't had to lift her office from her by force. His oath was to Epo as much as to the Speaker, but he was almost sure he didn't have the courage to do that to her.

As the door closed, Chesra sighed hugely.

Kimban looked around for a chair, but of course there was none. The single room of the House of Preparation was furnished only with the table on which their ceremonial garments were placed, a few floor mats for meditation, and the blanket padded shelf that served for supine exercises.

"Here, you'd better sit down," Kimban said, leading her toward the shelf. He was alarmed by how willingly she accepted that. He knelt to chafe her bare feet and calves. The chill he felt in her flesh pained his heart. But what almost undid him was the feel of her hand on his head.

"Kimban, thank you. This pregnancy has been harder than any of the others. I don't know what's come over me."

"After the baby is born, the village will call you to Speak again."

"I hope so." She stared into space. "If only my sister hadn't died."

If only her sister hadn't married Briller, of all the muck-eating excuses for a man!

Tears filled Chesra's dark blue eyes. The fire burning high in the hearth was reflected in her pupils. "If only my first born hadn't been taken by the—" She forced out the last word. "—Flints." She stifled a sob in both hands.

The Flints called themselves the Flintedged Warriors, a desert nomad tribe that periodically raided villages like Epo for children to sacrifice to their abominable gods. They had taken Chesra's first born by Briller just after she'd weaned him but before she turned him over to his father. Chesra had felt obligated to produce another son by Briller to continue the line of her sister's blood through her sister's chosen man. But then Chesra had two daughters, and only now, a son.

Gently, Kimban said, "You love your children, I know you do. When this boy is born, you will choose a wife for Briller, and your obligation to your sister's line will be finished. Then you can devote yourself to your daughters. One of them is bound to follow you as Speaker of Epo."

He had meant it as encouragement, but Chesra's sobs increased. There wasn't much time left before the Speaking. Kimban went to the table and brought Chesra's ceremonial sandals and his own silver sword. Buckling the sandals on her feet, he stood over her with the sword squared before his face and intoned the opening words of his protection.

She flicked her hand at him, as if to deny readiness, but he raised the chant higher and began the ritual passes over and around her, warding her person from untoward influences, spinning a silver blur of protection about her.

The sword was fully charged and moved as if cutting stiff dough, not air. Nobody in Epo but Kimban was trained and conditioned to handle these energies, and he had to make sure the sword never touched Chesra, for it would surely kill her. Yet the invisible light it wove about her protected her now and for hours hence against disruptive forces. Kimban was proud of his skill, learned in the Guildhouses of the far seacoast, the same Guild that trained the Speakers.

"Stand forth, Speaker of Epo," he finished, "and serve your people."

Eyes squeezed shut, she scrubbed tears from her cheeks, composed herself and rose.

He whispered, "Fasting is bad for you now. We'll finish this job, then break fast, and everything will seem better."

As the sound of eight marching feet approached she replied, "I truly hope so."

The escort was led by Briller, who performed with drilled precision. They walked the length of the village's main street under the full moon at its height. The soft light clothed the mud brick, tile roofed buildings in beauty. The street had been cleansed of horse droppings and raked smooth for their progress. Their colored robes seemed far richer than they were, and as they approached the only other wooden building in Epo, the Speaking Hall, they heard the assembled villagers singing the opening chants.

When the sound engulfed them, Kimban noticed Chesra begin to focus on her work. Each month she had performed routinely even during this pregnancy. Yet now, Kimban felt her summoning courage, high intent, and the deeper inward powers one brought to a difficult initiation. *Something's wrong, and she knows it. That's what has upset her so.*

Resting his left hand on his sword hilt, he prepared to face a test. He banished flittering thoughts, let his knees flex, loosened his joints and looked for the intangible forces in the air. By the time they reached the double doors of the Hall, he could almost See the subtle stirring of a threat. *How could I have missed this?*

But it disappeared when they entered the Hall which he had warded earlier. *Nothing can touch us here.*

As they passed through the several hundred assembled villagers, the musicians fell silent and the peace within the building was almost palpable. It would be a good Speaking.

The Hall was just an open space around a dais which was raised above eye level of the standing crowd. The dais was surrounded by a circular hearth made of river stones and laid with fire wood.

Above, a vent was arranged so the smoke from the fire converged above the head of the person standing on the dais. The air guides that achieved this appeared to be hanging decorations, but each was in fact magically charged. Attendants had raised banners of green and white instead of the usual purple and gold, on the rigging around the walls, so everyone knew Chesra would abdicate her office tonight.

Kimban planted himself beside the ramp leading up to the dais, and the escort bowed Chesra up onto the ramp. When she reached the dais, Kimban cranked the ramp aside, making sure the ropes and pulleys were clear of the fire's heat. Then he drew his sword which moved even harder here among the massed forces. Pointing it at the nearby tinder, he lit the fire.

The tingle erupted from within his own body, and leaped down the sword to explode as flame which spread around the dais. Then Chesra called out her invitation to the village to seek what they would know.

Forearms bulging, Kimban raised the silver sword, dancing now with its own light as well as the reflected firelight. Sweat stood out all over him as he labored to hold the sword high and open himself to the harmonic forces focused within the Hall. Then the sword emitted a fountain of silver light that caromed off the smoke baffles, then ricocheted down to illumine a villager.

That person had been chosen to ask their question, but chosen by what or whom, Kimban didn't know. It certainly wasn't him, and Chesra denied having anything to do with it.

Tonight, the first person chosen to ask for a Speaking was the most influential member of Epo's ruling council. "Is this the time to choose a new Council for Epo?"

The crackle of the fire filled the hall, then Chesra's voice came through, clear, steady and mellow. "No."

The sword's light danced and centered on another, a woman with two children beside her. "Is my husband alive?"

The pause was shorter. "Yes."

Kimban felt sorry for the woman, for no doubt she had planned to ask next month if her husband would return. The question she had chosen bespoke her love for the man who had been lost on a caravan carrying Briller's soap to market. When the caravan had been hit by brigands, only a few of the men had escaped being kidnapped for slaves. The incident had nearly impoverished Briller.

The questioning went on, some showing more wisdom in their choice of question, and some less. Occasionally, a seeker broke down at hearing their answer and had to be taken away. A rhythm developed, the kind of nearly musical beat that denoted a fine Speaking. Despite her earlier difficulty, Chesra was handling her job in superlative style.

And then, without warning, she screamed.

Kimban whirled. Chesra stood, eyes wide, fist to her mouth. Before he could extinguish the fire and lower the ramp, Chesra's voice cut the veils of power Kimban could See around her. "There will be flames of destruction, flames of war! Epo will burn at the hands of riders from the desert dressed in black, the Flintedged Warriors!"

She's flashed-back to the old raid. The Speaker's sanity was Kimban's responsibility. *I should have seen the signs. I should have lifted her office last month.* Sanity could become a delicately balanced thing, when one took the vows of a Speaker, but Chesra had always been so stable.

Sweat beaded Chesra's pale skin, and words ripped from her against her will. "Epo, hear your Speaker! The Flints come again. Even now they choose Epo from all the villages around the desert. In council they vow to supply their gods' sacrifices from your children. Under this sacred full moon do they doom your children." She drew breath, and Kimban Saw the forces swirl about her as she lowered her voice for an Active Speaking, shaping the truth as she spoke it. "But this time they *can be stopped!* This can be their last raid, ever. Your Speaker has Spoken." Chesra collapsed in a heap of robes, hair floating out over the fire.

With all his might, Kimban whipped his sword around and waved it over the flames before him. He felt the sword hilt heating in his grip, as it had the day he'd made it, then darkness spread from the point, extinguishing the fire. The moment a path was clear, he slammed the ramp down and scrambled across it, sheathing his sword.

He felt for her pulse, and peeled back one eyelid. *Alive.* Crooning the healing notes, he gathered her hair to the nape of her neck, then rolled her into his arms. He barely felt the strain as he lifted her like a baby. He charged down the ramp. "Get the midwife! Get the healer!"

Briller met him at the foot of the ramp, but Kimban strode past, heading for the door. Chesra's two daughters, Nina and Aith stopped him. Nina, the elder, yanked on her mother's robe. "Mother! Are you all right?"

Nina was barely seven years old. Her nurse pushed through the crowd and snatched the girl aside. "Don't—they'll take care of her as best anyone can."

Aith, however, hardly four years old, plastered herself to Kimban's leg and wouldn't let go as she sobbed, "Mommy!" She was wearing the long gray and blue shawl Kimban had knit for her. The nurse grabbed at the shawl, scolding, "Aith!" But she had her hands full with Nina, who was struggling to get back to her mother.

Suddenly, Chesra's head tossed. One hand flopped out of Kimban's grasp in a vague gesture toward the children, and the Speaker mumbled, "It's all right, Nina. Don't carry on so, Aith. It's going to be all right now. I have said...." She sighed back into oblivion, but

Kimban almost heard the last word, "...so."

Someone finally peeled Aith off Kimban's leg and he escaped. The air was cool, brisk and invigorating but Chesra didn't stir again until he had her ensconced in her own bed. As required of him as her Guardian, he removed the ceremonial trappings and performed his required duties over her, save that he could not bring himself to lift her office while she slept. Finally, he allowed the midwife and the healer in.

By then, Chesra was sleeping normally. Still, the two of them fussed over her until dawn, burning noxious powders in a brazier, and bathing her limbs in vile smelling things.

Dismissed from the sickroom, Kimban warded the house, as if it needed any further work after all he'd done on it, and retired to his own house next door. But he couldn't sleep.

The following weeks were filled with preparations for defense. The Speaker had Said they could win, but that didn't mean they would. Those who complained that she hadn't predicted certain victory were told to shut up or move to another village. What she had Said had nearly cost her life.

So they dug traps on the approaches to the village, and mended the village wall. It was a fort's wall, built for a King's garrison centuries before but still sound. The ruins of the garrison's stable and barracks were under the central square of Epo, but the village had maintained its wall. Now, supplies were laid in for a siege, and people were sent to the neighboring villages to buy arrows, burning oil, and any weapons they could. Envoys were sent out to find a village that would take their children in, so that come what may, at least the Flints wouldn't get them.

Word spread of the Epo Speaker's pronouncement that the Flints could be stopped, and a scattering of adventurous men came, offering to fight, but no villages sent real forces. Epo's Speaker was pregnant, thus unreliable. They decided to fortify their own villages, for the doom she had Spoken on her own village might actually pertain to another.

The Epo Council could not find anyone to shelter Epo's children. Many said that if the Flints had selected the children of Epo for their gods, then those children would be sought and taken wherever they hid. Nobody wanted to bring that scourge down on their own village, and no other village's Speaker would Say anything on the matter.

So Epo dug a cellar under a sturdy building and made a Safe House for the children. Three adults, too old to fight, were chosen to care for the children. Everyone else was armed and drilled for battle.

After he was sure Chesra was recovered, Kimban urged her to Speak the Abdication. But she argued that since the full moon was past, it was more dangerous to do it now than to wait for the next full moon. Besides, since there was no one to replace her, Epo would be without a Speaker when she abdicated. "Everyone else is preparing to take risks to save us all, why shouldn't

I? It will all be over before the next full moon, and there will be peace."

Nothing he could say would sway her, and indeed, the agitation that had gripped her before the last Speaking was gone. She seemed her old self, pacing about the village and quietly encouraging everyone in their efforts. Her very serenity carried the power of the Speaking Hall.

Serenity? Or resignation? Kimban wrestled with that, but still could not take up his sword and sever her from her office against her will.

One day, a delegation arrived from the distant village of Cantry. The Speaking hall was quickly arranged with tables and chairs. Chesra, Kimban and the Epo council met with the delegates all through one hot afternoon and into the night. They were curious about the rumors, but clearly had no intention of helping with either men or weapons.

Finally, in exhaustion and frustration Kimban rose for one last impassioned appeal, ending, "Should we succeed alone in defeating the Flints, all the villages at the desert's rim will benefit. How do you suppose our descendants will regard your descendants when your cowardice is known?"

By the stifled gasps from Epo's tables, he knew he'd exceeded his authority. But reason had gotten them nowhere, and Cantry was the only village that had cared enough to come to investigate. They *had* to be the ones to offer help.

In the shocked silence, the Cantry delegates

conferred, then the leader of the delegation, a stocky, grandmotherly woman clad in layers of gold jewelry, said, "Cantry can't spare any men to fight for you. We, too, have been subject to the Flint raids. However, we will send wood from our forests, arrows and swords from inland, and oils to make hurling-fire to defend your walls. That is all we can do."

That was the only concession Epo won before the delegates left, but Kimban overheard them talking among themselves and felt the tone of their comments had changed radically. They were determined not to be known as cowards.

Fretting and worrying, Kimban attended to his share of the preparations, not only carrying his silver sword out to the traps and warding them, but also peeling off his shirt and digging, hammering, and heaving with all the men. When Cantry's wagons arrived, he pitched in to unload.

Their best carpenter was a woman who specialized in cabinet making using woods imported from so far away that a man's weight of them could cost a year's profits from Briller's soap output. Now she supervised the construction of traps.

Kimban joined the crew using a rope and pulley to lower a brace into place after she cut it to fit. It went into place the first time, snug and exact. He had never been able to figure out how people did things like that.

They had just gotten the beam in place, and a group of youngsters were camouflaging the trap, when the alarm bell rang out in the pattern that meant *Flints coming!*

Kimban flicked a glance up the side canyon that led to Briller's borax mine, the secret ingredient in his soap which was unlike any other soap made. Since it was late afternoon already, the worker's wagon was returning, and as he watched it round the final bend onto the flat road across the arm of desert that led to the village, the driver lashed his six horses into a gallop, raising a plume of dust behind them.

"Let's go!" Kimban ordered the builders with him, and herded them all toward the walls. *Briller's on that wagon!*

Pausing by the high gates, Kimban yearned to slam them into place assuring his own safety, but leaving Briller and his men outside. *Coward! Or is it Briller I want dead?* Standing there waiting, scanning the desert to his right and the verdant hills to his left, for any sign of Flints, Kimban faced himself and found no trace of jealousy. He did not want Briller to suffer, he wanted only to keep Chesra safe because he loved her. *Is that why I can't lift her office? Because it would hurt her too much? Is that the real reason love is forbidden between Speaker and Guardian?*

Shuddering, Kimban watched Briller's wagon zigzag around to the eastern wall where the gate was, avoiding the traps. Kimban could See no threat anywhere—no line of black warriors, no hint of dust raised by numbers of horses—no magic energy. But he was sweating heavily, and not from the afternoon heat, when the wagon thundered past him.

Feeling like a charlatan of a Guardian, he nevertheless drew his silver sword, activated the power he'd set into the traps, and signaled to have the gates shut. He summoned all his skill, put all his will behind it, and sealed the gates, welding them to the walls in an arc of power that no one should be able to break. Maybe not even the Flint magician. Surveying the work, he realized that loving Chesra had not diminished his skills, but enhanced them.

As he finished, Chesra arrived panting from the exertion of walking. Seeing he'd finished, she wilted in defeat.

"What's the matter?" he asked anxiously.

"They were watching. Now they know how our wards are set and where the weak spots are."

He glanced to the northwest corner of the wall. He had done as they'd planned, yet he had betrayed his office.

Others clustered about them, and Chesra turned, resting her hands on her bulging abdomen, and told them, "I rang the alarm because the Flints have sent their magician's apprentices to scout Epo. They know we know they're coming—but they plan to come anyway. It's only a matter of time."

They had prepared for this, and the days of waiting went smoothly. But Kimban kept mulling over the events at the gate. If he really wasn't jealous of Briller, Chesra had Spoken falsely. She could be wrong about everything, and it was his fault. He began to doubt himself as Guardian.

Then, one night well before the full moon, the black clad warriors attacked. They made it to the walls, despite the traps, before Epo sentries spotted them. But then it was a pitched battle in which all the advantage was on Epo's side.

The Flint magician could do little against flaming oil cast down the stone ramparts onto Flint men. At dawn, Epo marksmen picked off the enemy one by one, confident in their ample supply of arrows. By noon, the Flints retreated.

While the Flints' magicians were busy treating the wounded, Epo unlimbered catapults and lobbed hell-fire into the Flint camp. When the nomads moved their camp back, a squad of Epo's youths slipped out an escape tunnel and released a gate which fed borax into the water supply the nomads would have to use if they stayed. It would taste peculiar, but they would drink it and their bowels would turn to water. But Epo did not want to chase the Flints away. They wanted a definitive victory.

"When we're sure they're weakened," the head of the Council declared, "we'll go out after them. Their horses won't drink much of the tainted water. Thirsty horses don't run fast. We'll take them easily."

The plan seemed to assure victory, and all was going well, but Kimban could not make his peace with it. A victory based on trickery just wouldn't feel right to him.

The night before their planned assault, Kimban couldn't sleep. He walked the wall, his silver sword shrouded in black velvet against reflection. Pointing the sword down and out, he felt for the rich warmth of the silver's response to his wards. He came to the node of the wards at the northwest corner of the walls, attention directed outward, and paused to study Epo's grain field, harvested a bit early to prepare for war. Beyond, trees rose out of dense underbrush, dark and threatening in the moonlight, but trenches and traps made it virtually impossible to cross that field. Weakest spot or not, they wouldn't attack here.

Low voices drifted through the silence.

"Of course you can do it, Chesra. You've given Epo enough years of service, especially now with your victory over the Flints. You can abdicate and become my wife, raise your own son, and your two daughters in peace. *Our* children, raised by their own parents."

"I love my children more than my own life."

"Then be my wife. Who would you choose for me, if not yourself? Who would you choose for yourself, if not me?"

The words sent hot daggers through Kimban's guts, and shamed though he was, he held his breath not to miss a word of her reply.

"If I had known how I would feel about my children, before I chose to become Speaker and give up all that, I might have chosen differently. If I'd known what it meant to bear children when I gave you my oath to provide you a son in place of my sister's son, I might have chosen not to do that even though you freely gave me your oath to let me choose your next wife. Had I known what all of this would cost me, I might not have had the courage to go through with it."

"But now you have me."

Kimban heard a smile in her voice as she answered, "You give great back rubs to bulgingly pregnant women."

"Only one woman—all the woman I want."

"I wish you'd stop saying that."

"I mean it. Please, answer me, Chesra. Don't you love me? Don't you want to be my wife?"

The pause was long enough that Kimban could feel her struggling between the Speaker's impulse to bald honesty, and the woman's need for emotional expression. He had been right. She should have laid down her burden nearly a month ago, and come what may, he'd have to get her to do it at this next full moon, or do it for her. He glanced up. Tomorrow.

She replied softly, "You married my sister, not me. I can't be her for you. I am and shall always be Speaker. But if I had not chosen to Speak, I might have chosen Kimban."

Caught in the grip of the overwhelming thrill of hearing his feelings validated, Kimban shuffled forward a step, then checked himself, embarrassed to intrude.

"What was that?" asked Briller. "Wait. I'll check it."

Kimban stepped into the moonlight, calling out the password. He saw them sitting against the battlements, shrouded in deep shadow, and saluted with his sword. "I was just wall-walking. I didn't know you were here,

Chesra."

A mean, calculating look twisted Briller's chunky features. "You knew. You checked her house, found her gone, and searched. What were you doing in her house—at night?"

The insinuation lit a fire in Kimban. For all that they felt for each other, neither had ever violated their oath. Gesturing with the sword, he forced words out between gritted teeth, "So long as I hold this sword—"

Without warning, forgetting every caution ingrained from childhood, Briller grabbed the shrouded sword, his bare hand closing on velvet. "You think *this* gives you license to—you miserable excuse for a man, you haven't Guarded her, you've seduced her!" He tried to wrench the sword away.

Kimban yanked the sword free, leaving the velvet in Briller's hand, baring the blade in the moonlight.

Briller swatted at the naked blade with his bare hand. "You've soiled this sacred—"

Briller's flesh welded to the silver, and white bolts of energy fountained wildly from the sword's raised tip. He stiffened, transfixed by the energies he was not conditioned to conduct. Kimban's own hand was locked to his sword's hilt, and pulses of shock paralyzed him.

He knew when the charge on the sword was exhausted, for he felt it shift and tap into the warding screen that flowed through the walls. Suddenly, the power ripping through them increased a thousand fold.

Briller emitted a gargling scream, and still Kimban

struggled to wrench the sword from Briller's grasp. Briller was an open channel for the energies which flowed from the highly charged wards to both the sky and the earth through Briller's own flesh. The more Kimban controlled its flow through himself, the more energy flowed through Briller.

Great jagged streaks of light flashed skyward with the cracking sound of lightning. In a moment, they'd both die.

Then, as abruptly as it had started, it was gone. The darkness that descended was more profound than any Kimban had ever experienced. He could not even see the sword before him. *I'm blind.*

"Kimban, help me!"

Chesra's voice. Feeling came back into Kimban's arms, and his eyes adjusted to the moonlight again. Briller was slumped over Chesra's legs, and she was struggling to get free. *She pulled him away from the contact!* Then, as thought began to flow, *She fell!*

Slipping the sword into its sheath, he knelt to heave Briller aside. "Are you all right?"

"Of course, but he—Kimban, is he dead?"

Briller groaned, head tossing.

"I guess not. But you—the baby."

"Never mind. The walls! The wards! Can you rebuild—"

He shook his head. She said, "Then I'll Speak them—"

"No! You'd have to make them from scratch, and that would kill you. I'll be able to do something soon."

But it was too late. Just as a squad of men trotted toward them, the thunder of horses hooves filled the night. All over the walls, torchlight sprang up, and below, the tolling bell roused all to their battle posts.

With an anxious glance at Chesra, Kimban trotted out to meet the sentries coming toward them. "You! Go back and get the midwife and the healer. You two, go defend the gate, and tell everyone the wards are all discharged. Get ready to fight in the streets. And you, man Briller's station."

Behind him, Chesra laid her cloak over Briller's supine form, and then came up beside Kimban. "Look!" She pointed.

Approaching the gate was a double file of draft horses escorted by dark shadows bearing torches. Between the horses hung a huge tree trunk. "Ten minutes at the most. I can't do anything in that time," admitted Kimban grimly.

"Don't worry about the gate," she said tensely. "There! Scaling ladders."

Now that she pointed them out, he could see the rows of men carrying the horizontal frames. The ladders and the battering ram were made from the trees that grew on the slopes north of the village—Epo's own trees.

"How could they have known our wards would fail? Their magician's not a Speaker."

"They have their ways, I suppose, though I'd never have thought Briller would be so stupid!"

Somehow, the other man's action was no mystery to Kimban. In his place, he too might have lost common sense. Studying the approaching force, Kimban ran to help move their defending oil pots into place. Shouting orders this way and that, he worked for what seemed like hours, striving to put determination back into the defenders. At the moment when the gates fell, he turned and ran back to the Speaker's side.

She was still on the northwest corner of the wall, struggling into her ceremonial battle cloak held out by a young girl with a crippled left arm. Turning, the girl caught sight of him, and her confident face went grave and expressionless. "I brought yours, too, Guardian."

Gruffly, he took the garment and flung it about his shoulders. It was welcome in the predawn chill. "Thank you, now get back to the children's hole, quickly!"

She left and the Speaker turned to Briller who was now conscious, sitting propped against the battlement with his face buried in his hands. Kimban didn't need any imagination to sympathize with the man's headache. *Another minute and we'd have both been dead.*

He tugged his eyes away from Briller, and stared down at the battle inside the walls. Epo's citizens were armed with swords, knives, maces, armor and other soldier's gear—but they had sparse training in their use. Still, the nomads fought wearing nothing but their black shrouds. Their favorite weapon was a wicked short sword. They all wore daggers, but never used throwing knives.

The roofs of Epo were manned by the smaller women and the youngsters too old to be targets of Flint kidnappers, but too immature to be any good at hand to hand fighting of adult men. They used bows, throwing knives and sling shots, dropping stones, and buckets of oil equipped with siphons to spray oil on the unwary so that fire-arrows could ignite them. All the wood in Epo's buildings had been protected by Kimban's wards, so it couldn't be set ablaze. Now, however, all those wards had been depleted of energy.

"I See little protection left for our buildings. There will be fire," announced Kimban.

"Can you work with the sword yet?" asked Chesra.

He drew the silver shaft. It was light and dull, but its charge was rebuilding. He flicked the blade about experimentally. It moved easily, as if it was only a silver blade. "Not worth much yet."

Something in the village streets caught Chesra's eye. Kimban saw a tangled knot of fighters atop the potter's shed, three defenders against one agile Flint with a gruesome scar on his forehead. Suddenly two of the defenders spun end for end and fell crashing into the street below where they were trampled by Flint horses. The Flint on the roof casually disemboweled the last defender.

"Dorset!" gasped Chesra in recognition.

Looking again, Kimban saw that the last victim was indeed the young man who had served Chesra as a houseboy during his childhood. As they watched, the Flint took out a jeweled dagger and ritually severed the boy's left hand, offering it up to his gods before pocketing it.

Chesra twisted aside, a strangled sound escaping her.

Then she tossed her head and blinked aside tears, her mouth a grim line as she focused on the battle outside the walls.

Wrenching his own eyes from the scene, Kimban hefted the silver blade, wishing it could reach the savage on the potter's roof. Then a scaling ladder thudded into place barely ten paces away. Kimban crouched, his sword coming up.

"You'd better find another weapon," advised Chesra.

Men who rushed to repel the ladder were cut down by the first Flint over the top. He was dressed in the usual baggy black pants, and belted tunic over which he wore a cloak pulled back and fastened to leave his arms free for his short sword. His head was swathed in a fold of black cloth that had a loose end trailing down the back of his neck.

With a stream of men mounting the wall behind him, the nomad sighted Chesra. As his comrades went to meet the defenders coming along the west wall, the first man came north, mowing down two men with casual flicks of his sword.

Kimban slammed the useless silver sword back into its sheath, and ran toward the attacker in a low crouch. While a third defender engaged him, Kimban snatched up the iron sword of one of the defeated, and came up on the Flint from behind. The man sidestepped as if he had eyes in back of his head, then his sword flashed between Kimban and the other defender whom Kimban now recognized as Epo's potter.

Kimban and the potter retreated before the nomad,

and Kimban thought he'd be forced over the edge of an embrasure, so unbalanced he felt with the iron sword that moved through the air without resistance. But he was getting the feel of it, using the same forearm muscles it took to work the silver sword, when Briller scuttled under their clashing swords, and came up with a weapon of his own.

Three on one, they pressed the Flint back. A gust of wind blew the man's garments about. Briller grabbed hold of a free end and tugged hard, intending to bring the nomad down. Instead, his headdress unwound and came free into Briller's hand. This left the man's hair and face bare.

A snarl split the handsome face, and suddenly, the Flint's sword was buried under Briller's breastbone. With a savage twist, the Flint freed his blade. Blood fountained as Briller collapsed, dead before he hit the ground.

Glancing about, the Flint retreated toward the corner where Chesra had taken refuge, his sword spinning a grisly wall of protection before him. Kimban hissed, "Distract him. I'll get behind him," and as the potter did that, Kimban rushed. But the Flint turned sideways to fight both of them. Still, Kimban was about to drive the nomad over the wall, when a piercing shriek erupted to his right.

On the wall near Chesra, was her daughter Nina, face red with tears, clothes torn. Her high voice floated over the clashing metal. "Mommy! They're in the safe house! They're gonna get Aith!"

At that moment, the Flint skewered the potter, shoved his body aside, and pushed past Kimban, heading straight for Chesra and Nina.

Kimban scrambled after him, while Chesra tucked Nina behind her. In mid-gesture, she froze, eyes locked on a point behind Kimban. The Flint followed her gaze, and Kimban knocked his sword aside, and slit the man's throat.

Kimban turned and saw the Flints' magician striding toward them along the wall as if he already owned the village. The magician's cloak shimmered and sparked in the fire lit darkness. He was broad, heavily jeweled, and his aura glowed like nothing Kimban had ever Seen before.

Kimban stood rooted to the spot, unable to conceptualize himself doing battle with such a one. Without warning, Nina ran out from behind her mother, and dashed across the open space to meet the magician with fists flying. Her little body hit the outer edges of what appeared to Kimban to be colored veils of flowing light, and slid sideways, momentum sending her up and over a merlon between two embrasures.

Arms flailing, she rotated in mid-air, horror infusing her features as she screamed. The sound followed her all the way down. It seemed to take forever.

Something inarticulate rose inside Kimban, and he knew he would kill this man even if he died doing it. Every last vestige of uncertainty was gone. It was more than his Guardian's duty. It had become the nature of Kimban.

He flung aside the useless iron sword, drew the barely charged silver sword and crouched. The magician shook his hands free of his robes and held them at the ready, as if they were weapons. Each finger was adorned with a jewel that glowed of its own light, each a different color.

Kimban knew nothing of the nomad's magic, but he knew the only way to stop such a one was to sever the silver cable connecting him to his body. Only his sword could do that—maybe—when it was fully charged.

To Kimban's surprise, when he advanced, the magician retreated, as if he took Kimban as a genuine threat. Heartened, he advanced down the west wall, hoping defenders could beat through to Chesra along the north wall.

But even as he stalked his prey, Kimban felt the battle ebbing, eyes turning toward the spectacle atop the wall. It was as if the world had drawn a deep breath.

The magician spoke, a bass rumble like carriage wheels on cobble stones, "I will take your Speaker, and wipe Epo from the earth. All will learn not to defy the Flintedged!"

No! Not Epo. Not Chesra. Never.

As he spoke, the magician struck, blinding cascades of light cracking forth like lightning, seeking to root in Kimban's body. Dancing back, Kimban flicked the sword, cutting each thread of light, and as the sword sheared through the energies, it soaked them up, glowing brighter.

His hand starting to burn, Kimban advanced, leery

of hitting the barrier that had thrown Nina over the wall. But now his sword resisted every movement, charge growing. It hummed, and he sang the note feeding it back, feinting this way and that, studying the magician's defense.

He felt fire ants crawling all over his body. Every pore was alive with pain. Searing brightness engulfed him. He was within the core of the magician's power and still advancing, still alive. Then the magician struck. Pain sheared through Kimban, driving him to his knees. A palsy gripped him, and the world spun. With both hands, he raised the sword, and though it shimmered and flickered under the onslaught, he whirled it above his head, showering sparks in a protective curtain about himself. Squinting through the layers of brightness, he aimed the sword at the densest part of the man's defenses, sending a cone of his own power to whittle a hole in that screen.

The moment the nomad retreated, Kimban rose and pressed on. Raising his forearm to shield his eyes, Kimban finally saw the cable he sought. Before the man could launch another attack, Kimban shifted his grip on his sword so he held it like a dagger. It resisted as if the air had turned solid.

The magician laughed, low, confident, chilling laughter, and Kimban felt lightning gather, killing lightning. Fighting the shuddering of pain wracked muscles, knowing he'd get no other chance, he flung his sword like a javelin, straight at the root of the life-cable, all his remaining strength in the throw.

He pitched forward onto his face, wholly off balance, and expected to be dead before he struck the stones.

But suddenly, the boiling energies vanished, and he was falling through clear air. He fetched up with his chin to the stones, hands splayed before him, barely breaking his fall, and when he looked up, the magician's empty corpse lay amid it's dull cloak and duller gems, the silver sword ashen black, standing in his belly.

Kimban crawled dizzily to his feet, and retrieved his sword. With one foot, he rolled the corpse over the inner edge of the wall. Triumphantly brandishing his sword over his head, he surveyed Epo's streets. The villagers raised a cheer. Then Kimban noticed his weapon was inexplicably light—lighter than silver could be. As he lowered it out of sight of those below, it crumbled to ash and smoke in his hand. Until it was gone, he hadn't realized how much a part of him it had become.

Chesra gasped.

He turned to her and found her backed up against the corner of the wall, hands fisted before her mouth as if to prevent Speech by force. Her eyes were wide, her face too white, pinched as if with pain. *The baby!*

As he went to her, a wash of sound rose from below. The nomads were retreating, and the defenders seeing they had the better of their enemies, were going after them more savagely than ever. Panicked, the nomads streamed out onto the desert.

Nearer to Chesra, Kimban could now see what she saw, revealed by the leaping flames of roof beams, wood piles and grain stores. The retreating nomads had cracked the defenses of the safe house, and had captured a dozen or so children to use as a shield as they retreated.

The Flint who had killed Dorset had a small, wriggling bundle across his saddle, a gray and blue shawl trailing to the ground. *Aith!* As they watched, the nomad made it to the gate and galloped through to freedom with a cry of triumph that could be heard over the battle.

Chesra thrust free of his protection and ran along the north wall, leaping bodies as she drove toward the gate and the escaping nomad. Kimban, weaponless, nerves burning from his battle, followed at a clumsy trot. When Chesra reached a point where she could view the fleeing nomads, she stopped and cupped her hands around her mouth, shouting to the heavens a Speaking that seemed to echo from the horizon.

"Hear this Speaking, who call yourselves Flintedged Warriors." Panting, she drew breath, and in that pause, the nomads slowed, mystified by the voice. "From this day, unto your sixth generation, you will yearn for and treasure children above all else, and be compelled to rut with your own kind under each full moon, but you will be infertile with your own kind. You will learn in frustration and sorrow, in destruction and blight and helplessness to bring forth love from your enemies and kindness from your captors."

She gasped, a wheezing, desperate sound, and suddenly Kimban knew her power was controlling her, for she had finally been driven beyond even her remarkable strength. He caught her back against him, whispering in her ear, "Don't Active Speak. Your baby will die! Chesra—silence!" But he no longer had the sword with which to remove her office.

She would not or could not listen. Words poured forth from her, and he could feel the substance of her very life gushing out with them as her voice, low and unstrained, almost melodious, boomed out over the desert. "As a sign of this Speaking, you and all your tribe will be marked with the horns of Nethe. All will know and shun you. Remove the horns, and you will labor six more generations under this Speaking. I, Chesra of Epo, have Spoken!"

With that, she wilted and Kimban lowered her to the stones. The nomads hesitated briefly, then wheeled and rode for the desert, abandoning their booty and the children.

Chesra's pulse became weak and irregular. Her lips and nail beds turned blue as she gasped for air, hands clutching her breast in agonizing pain. "My baby! My baby will die with me!"

"Chesra, let me try to save him. I will be his father. I will take a wife to raise him...."

Their eyes met. Before she loosed her last breath, she nodded. Then her eyes closed.

"Chesra!" *No. She's gone. Quickly!*

Hours ago, they had called for the healer and the midwife, but attack had come and they had never arrived. Now, however, those two had witnessed what had transpired atop Epo's walls, and made directly for their Speaker, even while others lay bleeding in the streets. Hastily, the midwife bent to the sad task, and long anxious minutes later, Kimban held a weakly mewling infant boy against his chest, sheltering him from the bitter desert wind, wrapping him in a shred of his mother's cloak. A tiny joy stirred within him, not quite smothered by the weight of shock and loss holding him paralyzed.

And then, with dawn misting the horizon, on the trail from the northeast, came a double column of men and wagons, heralded by the banners of Cantry. There would be help, and Epo would survive. Somehow.

Six months later, as Epo's rebuilding was being completed, word began to drift in from the desert that a strange new band of nomads had invaded the territory. They had black horns growing from their heads.

For nearly two decades after that, there was peace at the edge of the desert.

RUELLA AND THE STONE

A Royal Courier does not fail just because her horse founders.

Ruella trudged through a snowdrift, eye firmly on the darkening slit of the pass above her so aptly named Smuggler's Run. The trail was decorated with the remains of wagons that hadn't made it up the grade.

There was no King's Garrison guarding the top of this pass. The fort was on the other side at the bottom where it was possible to live through the winter. The wind howled at her back. The air was noticeably thinner up here. There would be no moon tonight. She had to find shelter, and soon.

An arrow whizzed by her ear and whacked into a dead tree to her left. She only knew it had happened after trained reflex threw her four body lengths to her right, prone behind a small boulder before her heart started to pound.

Nor does a Royal Courier fail just because someone shoots at her.

Her own bow had broken when her horse fell. One end of the bow had spiked into the swampy ground, the other lanced through the horse's chest as the animal fell. The freak accident had left her pinned under the carcass and she had used her sword as a lever to free her leg. The sword had broken. It shouldn't have—but it did.

She had her courier pouch, the Royal seal still intact, a few bars of trail food, flint and steel and a blanket in her backpack with the courier pouch. She had her knife and a blanket in her backpack. She had nothing to defend herself from an archer.

She plastered some snow on top of her fur-lined hood and edged her head out from behind the boulder to peer into the gathering gloom. Two more arrows plonked into the snow near her—too near.

Who would be sniping in Smuggler's Run? King Gorland controlled the lands on both sides. Bandits had been all but eliminated in the region. Could they be shooting at her?

She wore her Courier riding cloak, salvaged from under her dead horse and still smelling of swamp mud, but after the vigorous scrubbing she'd given it, the King's colors were clear. From a distance she could be identified as on official business. But as far as she knew she carried nothing worth killing for—a few accounting statements, a couple of personal letters, and a routine land grant transferring title from the Duke of Riverhead to his son that needed only the King's seal to go into effect.

Of course that's only as far as I know. But her duty was simple—to deliver the pouch to the King.

As the light waned, and the temperature dropped, she knew she had to find shelter or freeze in the night. There were caves that travelers used when trapped in this pass, and she knew most of them. So did the sniper, no doubt.

As the first stars ignited in the indigo heavens, she dared to peek around her boulder. And as she watched, way up on the steep side of the pass light flared into existence—it was a hemisphere formed by a coruscating rainbow of shimmering color. *Gods of the Talisman! A warlock!* It would be warm and cozy in that shimmering tent.

Who would send a warlock to kill a Royal Courier carrying nothing much of importance? Or more likely to stop traffic through this pass.

Who was not her problem though. Her problem was to get by him. And he—or she—was obviously prepared to spend the night up there keeping her pinned down until she froze.

In the gathering dusk, she took her bearings, estimated how many steps, spotted landmarks, and memorized a route to one of the caves that might shelter her and provide a way out through the mountain's old mining tunnels. If she was right, the tunnel emerged just above the Fort where she could get a remount.

And it wasn't the nearest cave which would be the first place the warlock would search. It was much farther away, and above the near one.

The warlock wouldn't be able to cross the snow-choked pass in the dark. If she could manage to move from boulder to boulder, not step where snow had accumulated, and stay under cover, she might be able to elude him even come morning.

At full dark she set out climbing the side of the gap along her memorized route, her hands and feet already going numb from the cold. There was only one really tricky spot where she had to leap, blind, from one boulder to another over deep snowdrifts masking who knew what hazards.

It was an insane chance—and she'd never have taken it if the sniper weren't a warlock, or at least didn't have a warlock with him or her.

She bent to feel for the edge of the boulder she stood on, sited on the rising stars to get her bearings, searched the blackness before her, and closed her eyes.

Taking a deep breath to steady herself, she reached deep within for the magic she had buried as a child. It was a power she never summoned, and always shunned when it roared to life unbidden.

Come on, just this once.

And the image of what lay before her flared to life behind her eyelids.

Keeping her eyes shut, she retreated three large steps, gathered her legs beneath her, focused everything in her on the flat top of the other boulder, ran and leaped into darkness.

Her boots clonked hollowly into the wind-scoured top of the boulder, slipped from under her and she sprawled face down, body curved around the rock. She lay trembling as her Vision sputtered away into darkness.

When she'd caught her breath she slid down the other side of the boulder onto clean gravel and scrambled up to the hidden cave mouth. If anything it was darker within.

With her right hand on the wall, she shuffled her way down into the cave, wracking her brains for an exact memory of how this cave connected to the mining tunnels. It better be the right cave!

"Nice night to spend by a cheery fire," said a deep, masculine voice.

Shock rattled through her nerves. But her hand suddenly held her knife before her. She backed a step away from the sound, crouching and preparing to die.

She didn't answer, and silenced her breathing as best she could.

The voice continued in a conversational tone, "But if you want a fire, you'll have to make one yourself."

She clamped her lips shut over the answer, sweeping the knife before her in a protective arc. Struggling to keep her bearings, she realized that the shaft that led out of the mountain had to be the one directly before her—blocked now by her enemy.

"You can relax. I'm not going to attack you. I'm not here to kill you. If I were, my arrows would have done the job."

She didn't relax. How could the warlock have gotten across the pass? There could be more than one.

Still crouched and moving the knife before her, she circled left, slowly feeling the way with her boot toe.

She found the opposite wall, and felt along it, hearing the other moving after her. She found a shaft opening. She felt the chisel marks of miner's work. Her opponent was still blocking the way to the shaft she wanted. She couldn't allow him to trap her.

Closing her eyes to summon Vision, she bolted down the shaft, flying at a full run down the slope into the heart of the mountain.

"Ruella!" complained the voice behind her, and she heard his boots ring on the stone as he gave chase. *I didn't tell him my name!*

He had teleported across the pass. He was no mere warlock, an ordinary person who gained command of Power through training,—he had to be a sorcerer born, and one who had earned high rank among the Oathsworn.

In a flash, her Vision showed him clearly—slightly taller than herself, he was dressed in the indigo and white robes of the Oathsworn, now spread behind him as he raced after her, anger on his face, power glowing around his hands. Alarm rang through her—the Oathsworn had turned against the King? *The Kingdom is doomed! I have to warn the King!*

"Ruella stop! There's a—"

She pitched headlong off the edge of the path into thin air. Trained reflex took over again and without her conscious will, she tucked into a forward roll, fist clenched tight around the hilt of her knife, blade away from her. Unbidden, her power flared as her fear of landing hard on jagged stone summoned it.

Her left shoulder struck first, a glancing blow that spun her off into a tumble and the next thing she knew she lay on her back, the courier pouch cushioning her spine, her right buttock screaming pain. Hot blood trickled sideways across her right temple. She willed herself to get up and run—anywhere, just away from her pursuer. But nothing happened.

"Ruella! Ruella-ella-ellaaaaa." The cry echoed behind her, around her, from all sides.

Move! she commanded her body. And it did. She felt herself jackknife to a sitting position. At the same time, her body-sense told her she was still lying supine across the rocks.

She was sitting, and she was lying down at the same time. Sitting, she could clearly see the tall indigo form edged in white before her, standing arms akimbo, an exasperated frown on his face. "Now why did you do that?" his voice came to her but his lips didn't move, and her ears didn't hear him. "If you hadn't levitated, you'd have died!"

A moment of shock was followed by sheer terror, and within the instant she was supine again, and not only supine, but dizzy as from a spinning fall.

I was out of my body. I was dead!

"No," the sorcerer contradicted her thought judiciously. "You were merely out of your body." His actual voice came this time from above and behind her.

"I was merely—merely?—out of my body! That's dead!"

Against her better judgment, she had replied to a

captor, opening a dialog where there should be none. Now he knew the level of her ignorance. She had handed him an advantage. She tested her body but it still wouldn't move.

"Well, no. Actually, that's awakening." With a shuffle-crunch, and a softly breathed curse he was kneeling beside her. "You were unconscious for a bit." He passed his ringed hand over her helpless body. The biggest ring on his middle finger was an Oath signet with so many rank jewels she couldn't count them. "Your back isn't broken. Slight concussion. Several cuts. Some bruises, mostly not from this fall."

With a mighty effort, she whacked his hand aside. She used the hand holding her knife, and the blade almost sliced into his forearm before his reflexes yanked his arm away.

"Good!" he said as he grabbed her wrist and twisted the knife from her fingers. Her hand refused to let go, and it took both his hands to wrench the weapon free. "See, you can move again. You're going to be fine."

He actually sounded pleased. He flung the knife off into the darkness, and she heard it land somewhere above her head. Mentally she marked the spot. Her Vision was still working, but she couldn't get a fix on the knife even though she saw the sorcerer clear as day.

Before she could regain much movement, he had stripped off her backpack, and had yanked off his belt and a scarf and bound her hands and feet. He trussed her up like a calf to be branded, though she struggled with what might she could summon. He was strong, not like your average scholar, but like a professional swordsman, with forearms to prove it.

He went through her pockets, confiscated a dozen small items. When he was done handling her like a sack of grain, she ended up half-slouched against a large stone, her feet curled back to where he'd bound them to her hands. He then perched on a nearby stone and watched her expectantly.

After what seemed a very long time of him staring at her and her glowering back, the cold eating into her already abused muscles, she broke down and asked, "So what next?"

"I told you. If you want a fire, you'll have to make one."

"But you tied me up and took my flint and steel."

"There's nothing here to use flint and steel on anyway except maybe your clothing, your blanket—or the dispatches you carry." And he now had the dispatch case beside his boot.

This man is crazy—absolutely mad. *What is going to happen to the Kingdom with a mad Oathsworn attacking the King's Couriers? Or maybe all the Oathsworn have turned against the King.* That wasn't supposed to be possible. The Oath bound them. Only a Royal command could unleash the power of the Oathsworn.

He raised one eyebrow as if he'd heard her thought. He seemed totally pleased with himself and absolutely happy to sit in the dark and watch her.

She knew that she had a small talent for rudimentary

Magic. She'd been tested as a child and been told she could have a career as a healer's assistant, but would never be able to do more than that. That decree had set her apart from her age mates, ostracized by those who had been her friends—viewed with fear and suspicion. Her parents had prepared to send her away to be schooled by the warlocks and mages.

And then one late autumn day, she'd been fleeing her friends bitter rejection, running fast and wild into the hills where the goatherds drove their flocks in summer. And she'd taken a fall—hit her head hard. The next thing she knew she'd awakened in a healer's cottage, reeking of goat piss and vomiting every time she tried to move.

Three months later, the Oathsworn declared her talent gone, wiped out by the fall. And the town had accepted her again. She'd trained, and worked, and sweated and made it into the Royal Couriers, ignoring and refusing every flash of her talent that tried to re-emerge. And she had never told anyone about those flashes.

Now, somehow the Kingdom depended on her ability to summon that talent, untrained as it was, and get away from a trained sorcerer, either a renegade or representative of the Oathsworn, a man who had probably crossed the pass with a spell and a casual step and could read her mind at will. The King has to be told the Oathsworn can't be trusted.

She let her Vision sharpen and searched the area around her. Meanwhile she grasped a small jagged stone that lay behind her and curled her wrists to bring it against the bonds. She was just barely able to move the stone against the material. Her wrists seemed to be bound with his scarf. Maybe the material would fray. *It'll take hours.*

"So, what's your name?" she asked, trying to keep her mind off what her hands were doing so he wouldn't notice.

"Gwinn of the North Steppe. You've heard of me?"

"No," she lied. "What have you done that people would gossip about you?"

Her plan was simple. Keep him talking, keep her plan underneath her mind so he maybe wouldn't notice until it was too late, get free then run like hell's beasts were after her. It wasn't a very bright plan, considering that her feet were already going numb and her hip might not take her weight in a slow walk nevermind a full run.

"I'm the one who led the King's men in the final assault on King Forsin's castle. I levitated two hundred men in full gear over the battlements in the middle of a blizzard—that I had caused. King Gorland awarded me the distinction of being Gwynn of the North Steppe because the Oathsworn can't accept medals or wealth."

Now things began to make sense. Here was an Oathsworn sorcerer bitter for the loss of worldly wealth and power required by the Oath. Thwarted ambition could drive anyone crazy—and the most vulnerable were those with the most talent and intelligence. If not for his Talent, he could have become a great General, been knighted, perhaps even been made a Baron and given lands. Instead he would die in sworn poverty, with nothing to leave to any children he might have. Talent usually wasn't inherited.

"I'm afraid I don't keep up on the war news from the North. My territory is the west coast and the trading routes beyond. So Forsin finally fell? Tell me about it."

He began describing the battle campaign that had led to his moment of glory. She gazed up at him in what she hoped passed for adulation instead of the abject terror and creeping dread for the Kingdom that she really felt. The Oath was imposed on the Talented at the first sign of their power for very good reasons. Without that compulsion, they could easily take over the world.

Meanwhile, the stone she held in her fingers grew warm as she rubbed it against the fabric that held her. I wish it had a sharper edge. Her whole inner world narrowed to the stone, one common stone the hope for saving a Kingdom from a mad sorcerer.

The palms of her hands tingled where the stone touched. Its surface began to feel almost soft. Then the rough stone surface hardened to a glass-smooth finish, like chipped obsidian. Suddenly the strands of material began to part swiftly with each stroke of the stone's edge.

He was describing how he'd gotten the idea for breaking the siege stalemate at Forsin's castle embellishing with technical details of how he'd discovered a way to use witchlight to grip minimally talented ordinary soldiers and channel his own power through their minds to levitate them. And then he discussed at length what Forsin's Oathsworn might have done to counter him.

She interjected a few encouraging comments, and in a bit he was pacing and gesticulating as he described the military contingencies, and how he'd argued the commanders into going along with his plan. He explained how he'd had to work to attain the Royal command he'd needed to proceed.

The material around her wrists parted, and it was all she could do to transform her grin of triumph into admiration for his genius. The stone was quite warm in her hands now, creating enough heat to un-cramp her muscles. She teased apart the loop that had bound her wrists to her ankles. It was hard to mask her effort. Then she started on the leather strap binding her ankles. She could barely reach it, but dared not move.

When he paced away, for a moment his body turned away from her and she used the opportunity to shift and squirm until she could reach the leather strap with the stone.

"And it turned out that you were right and the commanders were wrong," she offered ingenuously.

"Yes, and it wasn't the first time I'd been right, though it was the first time I'd managed to gain the audience I needed to get my plan accepted."

"And then you won the battle."

"Well, not single handedly. Nineteen good volunteers died in that assault. They were brave men to submit themselves to my manipulation. You see, to levitate them like that I had to get into their minds and use some of their own latent powers for them. And those who survived were never the same again."

And he got Royal authorization for that?

She felt a groove forming in the leather strap where she sawed at it. "They were changed? How?" She had not heard anything about that. Rumor had it that Forsin fell to Gorland's forces after a duel between two Oathsworn.

"Their powers were awakened and they were sent to be trained as warlocks."

They would be dead to their families. They'd lost everything they held dear.

"But it wasn't just my method of levitating them that did it. After they got me into Forsin's castle, everything went wrong. In moments I was faced off against Ian of Lessing in Forsin's courtyard while the battle raged around us. The truth is Lessing had me overmatched. I had to kill him or die trying."

He stopped his pacing and turned to inspect her. She held very still, focusing her whole attention on him and his tale. She held the stone pressed against the leather strap still.

"I was too frightened to consider the side-effects of what I did—I simply acted reflexively. I brought down power and blasted Lessing with everything I could muster. I didn't expect it to be enough. I thought I would die there, but maybe the men would be able to finish him off if I managed to do enough damage.

"I was wrong. When I hit him, Lessing died instantly.

He'd been gathering energy to fling at me—and what he'd gathered went wild. Contained by the bespelled courtyard walls, the energy penetrated every soldier there. They seemed to turn transparent—I saw their bones through armor and flesh. When it was over, some had died and some … had to be trained as warlocks to gain control of their new power."

What to say to a madman who confesses weakness? She gulped and scrabbled in her mind for words of praise. "But we now own Forsin's lands, and his eastern border which is defensible. The Kingdom will be safe for generations because of what you did."

He stared at her, her Vision showing him limed in a shredded aura of rose and gold. He turned his back and kicked hard at a rock, sending it across the open space. "Yes, it will be. But at a terrible cost."

At that moment, the leather strip parted beneath the stone blade. Without thinking, she stripped the bindings away, scrambled to her feet, grabbed up her backpack and sprinted for a dark opening far to her right that she had studiously ignored while she sawed at her bonds. Pain flared in every joint, her stomach revolted, her head pounded, but she drove her feet forward by an act of sheer willpower.

She heard him start after her with a shouted, "Ruella! No!"

Then she was into the side tunnel running like the wind. She took another branching tunnel with chiseled walls that slanted down. Veering left then right along the twisting way, she lost her bearings, no longer having any sense of where the tunnel that led through the mountain would be.

She heard water dripping somewhere. The air had become very still, heavy with an unscented dankness only found in the depths of caves. She was trapped down here with a madman who had persuaded a Royal to back his harebrained plan, killed a fellow Oathsworn instead of merely defeating him, been dissatisfied by the King's reward, and now was attacking Royal Couriers.

I have to get out and warn the King. I have to.

She paused at an intersection, sides heaving. Considering which way to go, she slipped into her backpack straps, feeling the weight of the dispatch case and her blanket against her shoulder blades. Distant echoes from every direction indicated he was still pounding after her, shouting her name as if pleading with her. She'd never dealt with a true madman before.

He had waylaid her, taken her dispatch case, then told her the tale of his greatness. Had he intended to rape her eventually? Or just murder her? He considered himself a tactical genius. He must have some plan for bringing down the Kingdom. If she could thwart that plan by making sure he never found the dispatch case, she would—even if it cost her life. *If the Oathsworn—or even just this one—have broken free of Royal command, we are all doomed.*

She picked a direction she only hoped might be toward the exit she sought and plunged on down into the mountain. Down and further down she went. The only warmth in the miserable damp came from the stone in her hand. Now that she could see the stone, she noted that it glowed right through her flesh.

It was a beautiful amber where it protruded between her fingers, polished and faceted like amber colored obsidian. And as she gripped it, her body was warm enough, her pain bearable. And she could see though only with Vision, sans color. She could see better than if she'd carried a torch.

She spotted a narrow slit to her left. It didn't look like a mining tunnel, but just a flaw in the rock structure. What was left of her sense of direction hinted that maybe that slit would connect to the shaft that led through the mountain.

Behind and echoing all around her, footsteps and panting, cries and imprecations made it clear the madman was gaining on her. He would be much too big to fit into that slit in the rock.

She took her backpack off and turned sideways, taking a deep breath to hold her stomach in, scraping her already torn riding leathers as she squeezed through the slit. Her right breast screamed where she scraped the nipple.

Then she was through and sidling down the narrow crack. She pushed herself to the fastest pace she could manage, not allowing herself a second to rest. With a sorcerer's magic, he could pry her out of here—or levitate the dispatch case out and leave her to die, trapped. He'd need time to do that though. He'd have to conjure help—or maybe his witchlight could do the job.

At one point the crack widened and she began to hope. But she reached a spot where the ceiling had fallen. A wall of rocks cut off further progress. Above her the natural crack stretched beyond her Vision into a tall chimney. Could that be light at the top? It was night outside, maybe not quite pre-dawn on a moonless night—but lighter than in here. Her Vision showed her nothing in the darkness above.

She considered retreating the way she'd come. But then she caught a glimmering of witchlight behind her, a pale blue ball of cold fire—had sent a search-ball after her. It mustn't find her. There was no telling what it might do to her mind.

She tucked the beautiful glowing stone into her bosom, braced her back against one side of the crack and the soles of her boots against the other side and inched upwards. The backpack protected her shoulders somewhat, and she was able to make it well up into the vertical chimney before her thighs were trembling too much to continue.

She stopped to rest and realized she had come so far that if she fell, it would probably kill her even if she cushioned her fall by levitating again. *And maybe I can't do that again!* If she fell and died, it would leave the dispatch case to the King's enemy.

Far below, she could see the ball of witchlight searching for her.

She wasn't sure where she was, but she knew exactly where she needed to be—where she'd expected to come out when she'd entered this cave—lower down, on the other side of Smuggler's Run, not far from the fort that guarded the road, though the pass was no longer a border.

While she tried to pant silently, she imagined where she thought she was, and where she wanted to be. Could she hold herself up here until the witchlight died then get down and sidle back through the crack? If she could, would she be able to find the way through the mountain and out the other side?

She had done it once, and she knew how she'd gotten here from the main entrance. The only trick would be climbing the cliff she'd fallen down. She could find her knife, slice the blanket into strips, make a rope. She could do it.

Back near the entry, where he'd first spoken to her, if she'd gone straight ahead, right through him, she'd be on the trail to the exit right now. Or she'd be dead.

Don't even think that! she scolded herself. A Royal Courier does not fail merely because she got lost. On the other hand, a Royal Courier trains long and hard so as never to get lost.

Below her, the blue witchlight flared brightly, and flickered as if signaling its master.

She began to inch upwards again searching above for any sign of an opening or ledge where she could rest or hide.

In the distance, she heard a rumbling crunch, and the soles of her feet and her flanks vibrated with some catastrophe. It happened again, and then again. She started to slip downwards as the rock vibrated and seemed to separate a little. Her thighs were aching ominously, her calves trembling. Her palms sweated, slipping a little more.

Dust billowed upwards from below, but didn't quite reach her. It obscured the throbbing ball of witchlight.

And then Gwynn of the North Steppe appeared amidst the cloud of dust, coughing and beating at his clothes. He stopped and recaptured his witchlight, absorbing it into the palm of his hand as he looked upwards. "Ruella?" He wiped dust from his face and eyes, then squinted upwards again. "Ruella! Come down from there!"

He shook his head, dried his palms on the seat of his pants, and climbed a newly tumbled boulder. When he braced one foot against the far wall of the chimney, she panicked.

She raised her gaze upwards into the dark above her and put everything she had into climbing that chimney. *I have to get out of here! I have to get out of here!* There had to be an opening at the top. She made it a chant, gasping in one more breath with every "out" and shoving with all her might on every "here!"

The amber light from the stone glowed through her heavy winter clothing, cast its warm light on her face, and arrowed into a beacon that pointed straight where she was looking, upwards. She refused to look down to see if he was following her. But she could hear scrapes and whispers between grunts and curses.

I have to get out of here!

The billowing haze of stone dust from below caught

up with her, dispersing the amber light, hazing everything. Her eye was focused on the point of light she could see at the end of the amber beam, and her whole mind narrowed to that one consideration—out!

She thrust upwards once, twice, three more times, and knew she was out of strength. Her body knew she was going to fall. But her mind gave one more thrust upwards. *I have to get out of here!*

In a dizzy amber whirl, she was suddenly seated on damp grass, crisp and brown with winter. In the far distance, across the valley the sun was rising. A few hundred strides below her the old fort stood staunch guardian of the road.

To her left, the road down from the pass wound around the last of the boulders and cut across the late fall meadow to the Fort. The Guardhouse on the other side of the road from the Fort stood empty and moldering in these peaceful times. Smoke curled lazily up from the Fort's kitchen chimney. The smell of baking bread wafted on the zephyr breeze reached her as a chevron of migrating geese passed overhead.

Behind her and all around the mountainside was steep but smooth—not a sign of an opening from a rock chimney anywhere. But far to her right there was an outcropping that might mark the mining tunnel exit she'd been yearning to reach.

The air was crystal clear, cold through which the pale shafts of fall sunshine made delightful warm spots. It was all so vividly real, indisputably and obviously real telling her she'd wakened from a very bad dream.

It was a nightmare. None of it really happened. *But how did I get here?*

Gradually she became aware of the warmth in her bosom. She dug out the amber stone. It was even more beautiful in the rosy sunlight. And if it was real, everything else was real.

"But what happened?" she heard herself ask out loud.

In that same moment, there was an inaudible pop—not a sound really—a displacement of the senses somehow.

And beside her, likewise seated with knees bent and feet flexed as if to brace against the wall of the chimney, was Gwynn of the North Steppe.

"Good Gods of the Talisman, woman, I didn't know you could do that!"

Ruella scrambled away and rolled to her feet running for the fort.

Three steps later she was on the ground, face down, with him on top of her.

He rolled off before the moment she felt his full weight—as if trying to avoid hurting her.

"Will you stop running!" he scolded.

"What did you do to me!" she demanded, forgetting she was handling a madman. "How did you send me here!"

"I didn't do anything to you. You teleported yourself and dragged me with you when I reached your exit point—you left it open behind you!" He glared as if offended by her carelessness.

She fisted her hands on her hips and yelled, "I couldn't possibly teleport anything! I have no Talent worth measuring, you nitwit! You're the sorcerer! You did something to me!"

"I did not!"

They glared at each other as the sun rose and the Fort began to stir to life.

Finally, he folded his arms over his considerable chest and eyed the glowing amber light at her bosom. "If you didn't teleport us out of there, then why is that focus-stone glowing?"

She fished it out of her cleavage saying, "It's not a focus-stone, it's just a piece of obsidian I found to …."

The lump of stone lay in her palm as if created to be there. She had seen a focus-stone once. It had looked something like this.

"Ruella, you made that focus-stone the way every Sorcerer makes their first one—out of an ordinary piece of stone. You made it because you needed it. I made you need it so you would make it. I didn't expect you to cut loose and run away. I didn't expect you to get trapped and teleport out. Teleporting is supposed to be the last of the twenty-two lessons in Sorcery, not the first. You are a very highly Talented Sorcerer."

"No." But she had no reasoned arguments to back up her claim. "What do you mean, you made me make it? What have you done to me?"

"I only tied you up like that so you'd feel trapped and desperate enough to access your Talent. I haven't done anything to you—believe me I learned my lesson with the King's soldiers."

What? "You tied me up to make me feel.... Why! Why would you attack a Royal Courier? How could you? You shouldn't be able—"

"I didn't attack you!"

She felt her eyebrows rise, cracking the dust caked to her forehead and showering it into her eyes. "You shot at me, you prevented me from getting through the pass, you chased me into the cave, you grabbed me and tied me up, then chased me up a rock chimney. But you didn't attack a Royal Courier?"

"Look, I'm cold, and we're both tired and hungry. Let's go get some breakfast at the Fort and send your dispatch case on with another Royal Courier so I can get you back to the Enclave for training.

"I'll also have to send someone to close that rift you left. I can't spare the time. I have to get you under Oathbinding as soon as possible. It's not that I don't trust you. It's the law, Ruella, for a very good reason, not just that you might abuse your power, but that you don't actually know how to use it safely." He cast a worried glance back at the mountain behind them as if he knew exactly where the rock chimney was.

She still couldn't take it all in. "You're not trying to steal my dispatch case? You really weren't trying to kill a Royal Courier? To bring the Kingdom down?"

He threw his head back and laughed, a hearty, full throated laugh radiating honest affection and admiration. "Ruella! Is that what you thought? No wonder you were so desperate to get away that you teleported!

But that just proves your loyalty to King Gorland. You are absolutely perfect."

"You weren't reading my mind?"

"Well, not after you made the focus-stone anyway. You developed a very effective shield using that stone."

"It isn't a focus-stone. I'm not a Sorcerer."

"Yes, it is."

"No it isn't." *Yes, it is and I don't know who I am any more. I don't know who he is.* "Why did you shoot at me? Why did you do this to me?"

"The King's orders, how else? I am Oathsworn after all. He needs eight new Royal Sorcerers on the North Steppe within the year to secure Forsin's lands. So he needs to discover adult sorcerers. Children just won't do. These Sorcerers have to have tested and true loyalty. Where else but the Royal Couriers would I find such? You, Ruella, are number four of the eight that I have induced to possess their native Talent. Now, unless you plan to materialize me a hot breakfast right here, you'd better come along."

He turned and walked toward the Fort leaving her to follow on her own—as if there were no question she would. As if she were already Oathsworn and had to follow his orders because he was her appointed teacher.

All night she had feared this monster. Now suddenly in the light of day, he was just a man—well, a Sorcerer of some considerable power and standing among the Oathsworn, not just a man—who practiced an infuriating arrogance. She no longer feared him. But she knew she would never, ever like him.

I'll bet he killed my horse just to set me up for this. If he did, he'll pay for it if it takes me ten years.

She settled her backpack and trudged after him toward the fort, warmth, and food, mentally plotting revenge.

ABOUT THE AUTHOR

JACQUELINE LICHTENBERG is a life member of Science Fiction Writers of America. She is the creator of the Sime~Gen Universe with a vibrant fan following (www.simegen.com), primary author of the Bantam paperback, *Star Trek Lives!* (which blew the lid on Star Trek fandom), founder of the Star Trek Welcommittee, creator of the genre term Intimate Adventure, winner of the Galaxy Award for Spirituality in Science Fiction with her second novel, *Unto Zeor, Forever*, and the first Romantic Times Awards for Best Science Fiction Novel with her later book, *Dushau*, now in Kindle. Her fiction has been in audio-dramatization on XM Satellite Radio. She has been the SF/F reviewer for a professional magazine since 1993. She teaches science fiction and fantasy writing online while turning to her first love, screenwriting, focused on selling to the feature film market. She can be found at her website,

www.jacquelinelichtenberg.com

And can be followed on...

twitter.com/jlichtenberg
facebook.com/jacqueline.lichtenberg
friendfeed.com as jlichtenberg